MY WILD LONE

Michael Adam

MICHAEL ADAM

MY WILD LONE

Woodcuts by ROBERT WYSS

He Walked by Himself . . . away through

the Wild Wet Woods, waving

his wild tail and

walking by his

wild lone

QUAY BOOKS

By the same author:
Wandering in Eden: Three Ways to the East Within Us.
Wildwood House, London & Knopf Inc, New York. 1976
Womankind: A Celebration. Wildwood House & Harper & Row, New York. 1979.

ISBN : 0 9512507 0 1

First published 1987 *by*
QUAY BOOKS, Quay Street, Penzance, Cornwall

Printed by ST. IVES PRINTING & PUBLISHING Co.
High Street, St. Ives, Cornwall

Eve! Magdalene!
or Mary you?
HART CRANE

Some names have been changed; some facts have been bent in the service of truth; some are even invented in the same essential cause. The rest is true as memory, imagination and the words that come can make it.

CONTENTS

WOMAN, IN THE PICTURE LANGUAGE OF MYTHOLOGY *represents the totality of what can be known. The hero is the one who comes to know. As he progresses in the slow initiation which is life, the form of the goddess undergoes for him a series of transformations: she can never be greater than himself, though she can always promise more than he is yet capable of comprehending. She lures, she guides, she bids him burst his fetters. And if he can match her import, the two, the knower & the known, will be released from every limitation. Woman is guide to the sublime acme of sensous adventure. By deficient eyes she is reduced to inferior states; by the evil eye of ignorance she is spellbound to banality and ugliness. But she is redeemed by the eyes of understanding. The hero who can take her as she is, without undue commotion but with the kindness and assurance she requires, is potentially the king, the incarnate god, of her created world . . .*

The meeting with the goddess (who is incarnate in every woman) is the final test of the talent of the hero to win the boon of love (charity: amor fati) which is life itself enjoyed as the encasement of eternity.

Joseph Campbell: *The Hero with a Thousand Faces.*

1 MISS BERYL

I give you the end of a golden string;
Only wind it into a ball,
It will lead you in at Heaven's gate . . .
William Blake

A BAREFOOT BELLY DANCER ANNOUNCES MY IMMANENT coming. Her breasts and hips are hung with pearls, but her belly is bare and swollen beyond the call of the dance.

Together with that and other fading photographs of my mother, I have a wand of dark wood with an embossed silver tip and handle, the legacy of my grandfather, a once noble Dane under the guise of *The Great Renville Roberty — Master Magician and Illusionist.*

A studio portrait shows him bemedalled in a black coat, a white tie and tails, standing upright and aloof against a painted landscape. In another he sits beside a small table with a tassled cover and a vase of artificial flowers, in Arabian robes, elaborately crowned; one hand upon the jewelled hilt of a curved dagger, his far-away eyes reflecting deserts. In another photograph, under another encrusted headpiece, he stares boldly back, his moustache wide with waxen ends, his bare arms crossed on his chest, circlets of old silver coins and of six-inch tiger teeth around his neck.

This great Dane roamed southern Africa with a wife from County Cork and a troupe of wandering players in a high, double-decked wagon drawn by sixteen oxen across the open veld between places and performances. In addition to the players, the wagon held scenery and costumes — all of the Dane's design and making — as well as other effects, essential stores and foodstuffs including, on one side, a long cage of chickens; on the other, a long cage of ducks. The troupe outspanned and camped at waterholes and by rivers. The Irish woman let the chickens and ducks run wild and, with clipped wings, free. The Dane unhitched the oxen, called them to the water to drink and wallow. Upstream, the troupe bathed and laundered. The Dane cut the top off an anthill, scooped out a stove for the Irish woman to bake bread, cook corn-porridge, eggs, potatoes, a chicken sometimes, sometimes a duck; or meat cut from a carcase that hung on the side of the wagon. When the nights allowed, the players slept with the oxen under stars of the southern sky. Sometimes, under the huge opal moon of Africa, lions roared.

The youngest child of the Irish woman and the Dane was born along the way. She grew sturdy in African sunlight; was soon running barefoot beside the creaking wagon; was soon learning her trade — dancing, singing, tumbling, balancing on a wire stretched between trees — under the exacting eye of her father, sometimes under his whip.

At five she made her first appearance on the stage. At fifteen — supple, bright and unschooled, mischievous, blithe, a buxom sprite — she already had the makings of a belly dancer, Fatima the Beautiful. And of much else.

At sixteen she sailed with the troupe from Durban to the port of Bombay, then crossed India in a railway carriage, emblazoned: THE WHAT NOTS: *Refined Vaudeville and Mystical Entertainers.*

The considerable cast comprised the five members of the Dane's family, each one playing many parts under many names. A Portuguese piano-player, a ten-foot python, twelve pigeons and other appurtenances in their several ways assisted. The posters promised Mystical Illusions, Black-and-White minstrelsy, 'High-Class Comedy,' Songs and dances of many nations, Acrobatics, 'Magic. Mystery. Music. Mirth.'

THE Apollo THEATRE

Special Engagement following their enormous success in China and Japan

" THE WHAT NOTS "

A High-class Variety Company and Mystical Entertainers comprising

" The Great Renville Roberty "

Master Magician and Illusionist, who will present his **GREAT EGYPTIAN BOX MYSTERY.**

" Miss Irene Beryl "

Serio and Ragtime Vocalist, clever exponent of classical dances. Come and see her in a dress of glass—simply wonderful.
Including the Famous
" HAREM DANCE "

" Charley "

Comedian and Siffleur. The man who made the King of Siam laugh, and last but not the least

" The Warleys "

In a most extesive repertoire of Comedy Sketches, Duologues and Dances.

Fatima the Beautiful swayed off the stage. The curtain came down. The belly dancer let the pearls fall from her, put on finest silk and as Dainty Miss Irene Beryl took up two long sticks attached to great sheets of the same silk. With such wings under a revolving spectrum of lights, she was a summer butterfly.

In other appropriate guises she did the Highland Fling, the Sailor's Hornpipe; waltzed in Dutch clogs, tap-danced and shuffled on sand to tunes out of New Orleans. In a flounced skirt lifted to show a little flesh between the black stockings and the white froth of underwear, she did the *can-can.* In another skirt, short, tight, shining black with a slit reaching high up her white thigh, she leaned against a Parisian lamp-post in wait for her lover, a sleek Apache — her brother Charley who, in another role had (the advertisement said) 'made the King of Siam laugh.'

Accompanied by Chopin, among trees after Corot, Miss Beryl became a *Sylphide* with small wings of wire and silk between her shoulder blades. Without support of this or any other kind, she then walked a high wire across the stage; came down to walk on her hands; tumbled, did splits and somersaults, turned cartwheels over and over to the *William Tell* Overture.

Later, with half her face white, half black, she put on a tophat, took up a banjo and with three others of the family and Sylvano Lopez, the piano-player, sang *Swanee River* and other songs of the Deep South.

Yet later, in a more northern, more lofty mood, in a long dress, with a feather fan and with soul, she sang of *Love's Old Sweet Song,* of the *Londonderry Air,* of *Trees* and of the *Roses of Picardy.*

Between times, Miss Beryl assisted her father, the Magician, in his *Black Arts or The Egyptian Wonders of a Thousand Years Ago,* lying in the air two feet above a table in a mystical trance — helped by a steel corset into which was fitted an iron rod joined to a lifting mechanism concealed by a black curtain. Behind this curtain her brother turned the handle: Miss Beryl rose. And fell one night when her brother was drunk. Still hidden there, Charley helped his sister to read and answer, blindfolded, questions put on paper by the astonished audience.

Miss Beryl curled up in a basket into which long swords were from all sides plunged; lay in a wooden box that was sawn in half by her father, and then by a wave of his magic wand and the cry *Abracadabra!* was miraculously made whole.

For her final appearance in *Artistic Living Pictures,* Miss Beryl pulled on flesh-coloured cotton skin. Bound to a pillar, protected only by Purity and a whisp of chiffon about her hips, she was a *Christian Slave in Ancient Rome,* encircled by tigers photographed by her father, enlarged to life-size, mounted on wood, cut-out, menacing. Within an eight-foot high, ornate and gilded frame, she was naked *Eve* with the live but well-fed python wound about her. With her arms severed above the elbows by the black velvet of the background curtain, she was the *Venus de Milo.* Then she was *Eros* of Piccadilly Circus, the God of Love himself, with bow in hand, balancing on one foot at the hub of the British Empire.

The daring of her seemingly-nude appearance was made acceptable, even elevated, by the artistry and at the end ennobled by patriotism — she was *Britannia,* with the accompanying piano promising that 'Britons never never never shall be slaves!' The Britons in the audience joined in loud agreement. For the last time the curtain came down. The audience clapped, cheered, stamped their feet. Some threw flowers. In Hyderabad, His Highness the Nizam gave Miss Beryl a necklace of real pearls. After a performance at the Kuen Seen Theatre in Foochow Road, Shanghai, a Chinese newspaper ended its long review: 'Never have such seen before. All people say very good. Plenty applause.'

At the end of one evening's performance in Calcutta, the dreamed-of tall, dark and handsome Stranger who had sat for several nights in the middle of the front row, stood at the stage door with an enormous bouquet of flowers. A little more than nine months later, and only six weeks after her last belly dance, Miss Beryl gave birth to me, backstage at the Strand Theatre, Jubbulpore. She was just eighteen. The war to end all wars had ended, and my father at the time of my birth was in England, in America, and elsewhere on biggest business. I was a love-child; what the old Romans called *terrae filius,* a child of earth; what Roumanians to this day call 'a child of flowers;' what some call a bastard.

With her child's coming, Miss Beryl made all her roles subservient to that of a Mother. Having an abundance of milk and motherkindliness, she gave her son *a taste for plenitude — the sufficiency that liberates from need and greed.*[1]

At first in a clothes-basket cradle, then barefoot, I went about India with the wandering players, the python and the pigeons; then sailed with them for Africa; then sailed back with them to India.

My father happened to be in Bombay at the time. He saw the poster, went to see the show again; again went with flowers to see the dancer he had once loved. More than once.

He found a two-year-old son.

My father and my mother married and lived at Alipore on the outskirts of Calcutta in the rented palace of the Rajah who had in happier times kept his soft, scented women there, amid banana groves and lemon trees. My parents lived well if not wisely. The will and imagination that went to make my father's considerable fortune seemed matched by an eagerness to be rid of it. Each Sunday my father would stand on a balcony and scatter coins to the multitude of beggars, *chokras,* ragged children who gathered there for the occasion. My father raced five horses, with the jockey Steve Donaghue sometimes in the saddle. My mother wore long lace dresses to the racecourse, with lace elbow-length gloves to match, a wide-brimmed hat, a tiny lace parasol held high. Win or lose, my father would afterwards give a party at which my mother might be persuaded to lift her dress and dance on the long table among the champagne glasses. Doubtless, my father drank champagne from her discarded shoe. It would be in character.

I learned of all this later. It was told to me, or was read in old newspaper cuttings, seen in old photographs. My own memories were few and for the most part unfelt; they could be called to mind, but did not call me. The India of my earliest childhood lay for the most part dormant and indefinite, but could erupt: the call of a rook in a Kentish wood would be echoed by the caw of an Indian crow; a small green hill in Somerset would of a sudden give rise to highest Himalaya, still, white, solitary, out of this world. Without prompting sometimes, in unlikeliest places, I would smell sandalwood and incense, frangipani, curry, jasmine and dung-fires in the evening of a Bengali village by a far-away river of long long ago.

My mother and father apart, only a few people of those early Indian years stayed to haunt me: one woman in particular, one man.

The woman was small, barefoot, burnt-sienna brown with midnight hair, a bright diamond in her nose: my Indian *ayah,* the nursemaid with me at all times, from waking to the edge of sleep. Years after, she would come with the closing of my eyes; all the dark and the warm animal smell of her. I would hear the silver tinkle of the bracelets on her wrist, see the swell of her dark breasts above the red *choli* when she pressed me to her because of some small hurt I had suffered, or for joy, or for no reason, suddenly. Behind my closed eyes she would come on bare silent feet bringing *dahl* and rice, lime juice, mangoes and lychees, caresses. She would again squat on the red Bokhara carpet sorting out clothes brought by the *dhobi-wallah,* singing all the while. Sometimes she danced for me again; her arms, her hands as underwater plants, afloat and swaying. Her head would remain upright and still, yet still moving from side to side; her black eyes remote, but on me all the while — alarmingly like the snakecharmer's cobra summoned from a basket to rise and sway from side to side, just so. In the silence at the end of an English schoolday, I would hear her feet slapping the stone floor of the verandah, her necklaces and bangles ringing out as she spun round and around faster and faster to fall at the end, breathless, laughing, on my bed, to lie on her back there, still, but for the lifting and lowering of her breasts.

Sometimes, more rarely, I would again sense that first meeting with Woman as more than mothering; not caring only, but *calling* in some beguiling, inexplicable way, as someone *Other,* as my *ayah* one night.

Was it springtime and desire in her pressed down and brimming over?

My father and my mother had kissed me goodnight and gone to a dinner party. The *ayah* closed and barred the wooden shutters as she had always done, but then, as she had never done, bent low over me in the shadowed room, smiled, brushed my lips lightly with her tongue, lightly in play. Then she pressed her soft mouth on mine. I was frightened. She pushed her tongue into my mouth. It folded, swelled, probed, quivered. I was terrified. That cobra's forked flickering tongue! Then she withdrew her tongue slowly, slowly. I felt loss. I put my tongue to my lip, expecting blood.

My *ayah* leaned back and away, laughed at my shocked, excited face, then spoke gently, reassuringly; patted and stroked me into calm again. Singing over and over four lines from a Hindustani lullaby, she sang me to sleep:

Nini, Baba, nini
Roti, machan, chini
Roti, machan hogya
Mehra Baba sogya . . .

One afternoon the *ayah* and I walked as usual on the

maidan, a wide green space in the centre of the city. I let go of the *ayah's* hand, threw my ball ahead, ran after it, stopped at the sight of a man sitting under a tree, naked, with black matted hair falling onto his shoulders, a string of marigolds about his neck.

The sight of such men had always moved me to awe, to wonder, to fear, to nightmare once when such a man strode into my sleep. This time I went forward to stop only a stride away from the rigid, erect figure. On the ground at the man's right side was an iron trident; on his left a small cloth bag, and a gleaming brass bowl shaped like a gourd. The man sat with crossed legs, one hand cupped within the other in his lap, his eyes closed. On his forehead a painted mark, like a great raindrop, ran down to the meeting of his black bushy eyebrows.

My *ayah* started after me but stopped short. She called me. I did not turn. The *ayah* called louder, insistently, 'Chota Sahib! Michael Sahib!'

The *sadhu* opened deep-set, dark enormous eyes; glared at me. Years after, I recognized the look in a book of Byzantine mosiacs created before Jesus was made in the image of man's misery — Christ in Majesty! Christ the Tiger!

Transfixed by fear, I could only stand and stare back. The *ayah* came no nearer, no longer called. The *sadhu's* eyes closed a little, looked kindly now. The corners of his mouth lifted. *Sadhu* and small boy faced one another, smiling. The *sadhu* bent his head, lifted the marigolds off his neck, held the orange circle up before me. I bowed. The *sadhu* placed the bright ring about my neck; let his hand rest on my head a moment. Then the *sadhu* straightened, unknotted his legs. He picked up the bag, slung it over his shoulder, took the trident in his right hand, the bowl in his left hand, then swung forward and up to stand tall and naked but for a small codpiece held by a chain about his narrow hips. He stood still, gazed down on me long and seriously. Then he smiled; then brought the trident, the bowl, and his hands together in salutation; then abruptly turned about, walked away.

My *ayah* ran forward, put her arms about me. I shook off her embrace, stood still and alone, staring after the *sadhu*. For all my *ayah's* urging, I would not move until the *sadhu* had crossed the grass to the *maidan's* edge; until he had, without a turn of his head, crossed the wide Chowringhee Road, heedless of hurtling trams and buses, speeding taxis and cars, bullock carts and rickshaws, the hooting, braking, shouting, cursing. The *sadhu* stepped onto the far pavement, disappeared into the crowd.

I refused the hand offered by the *ayah,* walked silently beside her, a little apart. She urged me to remove the flowers. I shook my head; wore the garland all the way home. There I put it on a chest-of-drawers, instructing the *ayah* not to throw it away, not even to touch it. For a few days the marigolds scented the room; then soured, browned, dried, fell apart. One day they were gone. The *sadhu* remained.

That the small dark woman who shared my earliest years should have stayed in mind and heart was not surprising, but why that one man of a few minutes of one afternoon so long long ago?

A grown man, I heard my father described as 'a large man in all ways; body, mind and spirit: a great sinner, a great saint.'

Perhaps it was the sinner that wished his son to be, if not saintly, at least respectable. Not yet six years old, I was sent to St. Paul's, a Church of England boarding school in Darjeeling, half encircled by the Himalayas, with the five white peaks of Kanchenjunga framed by the classroom window.

Not yet seven, I was taken to England and left at 'A Preparatory School for Young Gentlemen.' The means to the making of an English gentleman of me included cold baths at the dawn of each sunlit or snowy day, cod-liver oil and malt, Latin and French verbs before breakfast and, to ensure the healthy body essential to the healthy mind, innumerable games I greatly enjoyed. Our schoolboy souls were instructed by brief sermons at the start of each day, by longer ones in chapel on Sundays, by homilies in the classroom, at meal times, on the playing fields. A large framed copy of Kipling's poem, *IF,* hung in the corridor at a place where boys often had to gather, stand and wait. Each boy was urged at all times to be as Kipling's 'Man.'

I tried, but more naturally inclined to be as Kipling's Cat; the One that *Walked by Himself, walking through the Wet Wild Woods waving his wild tail and walking by his wild lone.*[2]

The sermons apart, I could not later claim to have suffered my schooling as so many great minds have done — because my mind was less or because of the ability, both given and learned, to be alone.

To the grace of that ability was added the gift of transposition, so that I could leave the appearance of myself in commonroom, classroom or chapel and yet be in Chimborazo or Cotopaxi or in the sunlit gleam of Popocatapetl;[3] could be swinging on jungle vines, or standing on some impossible peak alone, or stepping from a small boat onto a burning island with the wild gulls crying: Well come! Well come! Welcome!

Or, yet more simply: leaving the appearance of myself in the midst of many others, I could without a step or slightest effort, simply walk away, as Kipling's Cat, walking by my wild lone, as that *sadhu* of long ago 'clothed with the sky.' I would stand still in the midst of the crowd and see my own upright back move away, disappear into the far distance until there was no one, no one at all to feel lonely or feel lost in the crowd.

By such means, I survived my schooling to get my education after, elsewhere, in other ways — in large measure at the hands of women. I shed the sermons, forgot most of the lessons learned at school, but the women of those early years remained long after, dear and near as hand and thigh, mind and heart and wondering spirit.

When I came upon Goethe saying: *The Eternal Feminine leads us on,* I looked up from the book, looked back on my early years, stared at the sky, sat still, silent, wondering.

2 SHEELA-NA-GIG

Enter these enchanted woods,
You who dare.
George Meredith

BRIGHT AS THE SUN THAT SUMMER MORNING, MEMORIES would arise of the Serpent, of that first glimpse of the Apple; beyond the dark wood out of the long grass would rise the great house where Himself lived.

Whenever I heard the old old story, it was with recognition. But when I heard that it happened only once and long ago, I shook my head — it had happened in my lifetime. When I read that it had happened between two rivers in a foreign land far-away to the east, I shook my head — the Wild Strange Place was in the west of Ireland, beside a quiet lane, in the clearing of a wood on the edge of a great estate. I knew. I had been there.

I was in Ireland at the time because of the pity of a Priest for the small boy I was; six years old and left by my parents alone in an English boarding school before their return to India. The Priest brought me to his rectory home for three weeks of the summer holidays while he served in the parish of his father, himself gone on holiday.

It was an act of Christian pity that was not apart from the fondness with which the Priest sometimes lifted me onto his lap and laid hands on me, on head and shoulders, back and thighs; surprising me each time, for the Priest seemed at all other times distant, even indifferent. Such occasions must also have surprised the Priest for he would of a sudden seem to awaken to what he was doing, get up, push me from him. I feared his caresses even more than the fierce rejection that followed.

The name of the Priest was St. John Fitzgerald Sincock. We called him 'Mister Sin.' High, lean, hollow-chested, he hung above us in his black habit like a predatory bird. Smoke curled from his ivory-stained fingers. He sucked at a cigarette and the red glow lit the tip of his beak. After the hiss of inhalation, he sighed and instructed us in all the many sins. But of the greatest of these, it seemed he dared do no more than darkly hint. I wondered what it could possibly be.

After breakfast that summer morning, the Priest put long fingers lightly on my head, then turned away into his study, saying, 'Mind you be a good boy, Michael. Be a good boy, now.' Meaning: Do nothing at all at all for this day will be a hot one and the Devil abroad in his own climate. Unless I sat deathly still and dreamed no dreams, I had no idea how to be good, only how to be a six-year-old boy on a summer morning that was already huge with what might happen.

Anything could happen in Ireland at that time, for Ireland was innocent then. Slowly, stealthily, tigers in those days prowled the small islands in the still lakes; on stormy days they roared in the rhododendron bushes. Lions thrust gold barbaric heads through roadside hedges of fuschia, honeysuckle and wild rose. In lonelier, darker lanes Nothing could be seen and Silence was a hidden snake.

The Priest had said there were no snakes in Holy Ireland. It was a confession of blindness. Snakes were a matter of seeing. I, for one, knew that in County Roscommon at that time, boa constrictors hung at twilight like liana-vines from the trees, eager to embrace a boy such as I, at once alarmed and excited to be in the one world with snakes and steam-engines, volcanoes and rainbows, vampire bats, snow and licorice, grasshoppers, apes and elephants, Charlie Chaplin, Tarzan, travelling circuses, daring young men on the flying trapeze, hunchbacks of Notre Dame, redskins, gypsies, girls — even gypsy girls.

I saw her when she stood up.

Gypsies, I well knew, would steal a boy away, enticing him with apples and Garibaldi biscuits into their painted caravans, there to strip him and stain him all over with walnut juice, clothe him in rags to make a brown beggar of him. Even if he should ever escape, the door of his own home would be shut in his unrecognizable face.

My mother said that I never should
Play with gypsies in the wood.

But my mother was over many seas, unimaginably far away. For all the thump and dither of my heart, I did not turn back but walked on towards the gypsy encampment. A wolf of a dog barked and leapt as far as the rope about its neck allowed. A tethered horse and an old donkey cropped the grass beside a cart. A small man lay with great boots pointing to the sky, a check cap over his face. A thin dark woman stirred something — Irish stew? a Secret Potion? — in a black pot over a fire; while another, a giant of a woman with great breasts for the most part uncovered and with ginger hair, was throwing clothes over a hedge to dry. A naked infant on the grass nearby watched the little girl at his side build a tower of stones. Her elder sister stood beside a hooped tent of torn canvas and hessian sacks. It was she who, at the bark of the dog, had stood up. Now her small sister came to stand at her side; now her small brother stood beside. The man slept on but all others turned to watch me go by. The dog growled. I looked ahead to the hills. Somehow my whistle — a recent accomplishment — would not work.

The lane curved around a small wood. I turned in relief there, only to see a girl coming after me. I wanted to run but did not dare. It was useless to do so. The gypsy was older, had longer legs. She could, moreover, assume the guise of a snake if she cared, become a red fox, a black crow, even a high swift hawk, a wind even, invisible above and about me at any time anywhere, at all times everywhere.

I kept walking until she was at my back calling, 'Hey, little boy, hey!' I stopped and turned to face her. 'Where ye from?' the girl asked, staring with the dark eyes of a beast in a jungle book I had just read; out of a thicket of russet hair that lay dishevelled about her shoulders, over much of her face that was pale where it was not grimy and freckled. 'Where ye from?'

I did not tell. I pointed away from the Priest's house towards the town of Boyle where there was an old abbey and a church and shops and cars and lots of people and other priests and policemen and . . .

'All alone, eh?'

I nodded.

The girl smiled, 'Come', and turned into the wood to look for a walnut tree. Frightened and eager, I followed. She went barefoot, bare-legged through the brambles that tore at my socks to a clearing where a great tree lay on its side with orange fungus bursting from it. She went on into the shade of a standing tree and stopped beside a small pond. Half in sunlight, half in shadow, it gleamed like dark glass. The gypsy went down on her knees and, calling me to her side, stared into the pond. I knelt beside her and stared. The water was dark as walnut juice. All I could see was Fate.

Suddenly the girl thrust her hand into the pond and brought forth a frog, striped yellow and spotted rusty brown. She sat back on her heels, holding the frog by a thumb on its back. Slowly she lifted it to my face. 'Kiss it,' she commanded. 'I dare ye.'

I would grow warts all over and get leprosy or sleeping sickness or *beriberi* or go blind in one eye and limp on a wooden leg for the rest of my life . . . But I bent over the frog. I could see its small heart beating. I could feel mine. I put lips to the valley between the frog's eyes. 'Now you'll be lucky' said the gypsy girl, adding with a laugh, 'Lucky in love.'

She looked at me gravely a moment, then turned back and took her thumb off the frog's back. It leapt in a great curve from her hand. I watched the circles spread all the way to the other side of the pond. The girl turned, 'Like to kiss *me* now?'

I stood up, stared at her. What on earth would happen if I did? What in heaven would happen if I dared? Or in *hell?* I took a deep breath and nodded.

'Got a penny? It'll cost you a penny.'

I reached into my pocket, gave her a penny. She knelt down before me, lifted her face, closed her eyes. I bent over her, dared to touch her cheek with my lips. Her eyes opened wide. 'On the *mouth,*' she said. 'That's for a penny.'

She closed her eyes again, pouted.

I put my mouth to her mouth, lightly, then drew back. She shook her head in despair of me. 'Sure now, ye've never kissed a girl.'

'I *have'*, I protested, remembering a party two Christmases ago when I had been led by a grown-up under the mistletoe into the embrace of a girl, small as me, and as shy.

'Not really kissed a girl.' The gypsy shook her head. 'Not *really*.' She added, 'Here, I'll show ye.' She put her hands on either side of my head, took hold of my ears, drew me to her. 'I'll show ye how grown-ups kiss. My sister — she's wedded — she showed me.' Her thin arms slid around my head, her hands knotted behind my neck. She held me close, ran her tongue over her lips, put her wet lips on mine, then opened her mouth as though to swallow me. Held hard against her, I stared at what I could see of her face, enormous now and near. Her eyes were again closed. She seemed elsewhere. But her tongue was now prising my lips apart. My mouth gave way, opened to the thrust of her tongue that was now a dagger, now a bat fluttering about the cave of my mouth. Then her tongue stiffened again. Then it was still. Then it slipped from my mouth as she slowly unwound her arms,drew apart, opened her eyes again. I fell back trembling in the terror of first love.

Gently, as though from a great distance, the girl smiled on me while I gathered breath and being. When she saw that I had recovered, she put her head on one side, whispered, 'Like to see something?'

'What?'

'Ah! *Something*. Got another penny?'

I took another penny from my pocket, handed it to her.

'And another' she said. 'It's something *special*.'

I had no more pennies. I pulled out the linings of both pockets to prove it.

'Got another penny at home?'

I nodded.

'This afternoon then. I'll show ye *now,* but this afternoon ye'll bring another penny. Promise?'

I promised.

The girl stood up. Her dress, taken from some suburban washing line, hung over her narrow shoulders, reached far below her knees. She bent low and taking the hem of the dress in her hands, drew it like a theatre curtain slowly up her long legs. Her shin showed a wound with dried blood on it. She drew her dress higher, over her bruised knees, higher over her pale thighs to where they pointed to a mound of flesh like a small fruit, split down the middle.

I had seen nothing like it in all the world, in mirror, bath or bed. Indeed it was *Something,* as she had said. Something *special,* strange and wholly *Other.*

When the girl at last let her dress go, it seemed that a door had been slammed in my face. 'Now ye've seen, don't fergit — another penny, this afternoon, *here.'*

Lost in wonder of what I had seen, I slowly nodded. The girl laughed and ran from me out of the wood.

I sat on. My skin was white as ever. I wore the same shirt, shorts, stockings, shoes. I was free to go. But the gypsy *had* stolen me away; had put a spell upon me that I could not shake off; nor had wish to do so.

I walked back to the Priest's house, aware that it was from another world that I came. I sat down to lunch in fear of the Priest's questioning, but the meal was for the most part eaten in silence. The Priest seemed abstracted, as so often; his mind full of the morning's studies, of the Book he was writing. Whatever the Book was about, I was sure that it was not about gypsies, nor about girls, so that the Priest had no need of the knowledge I had gained that morning.

The Priest had to visit the sick of the parish that afternoon. When I heard the front door shut, I took a knife from the table, ran up to my room. I slid the knife blade into the slot of my money box, tilted it, emptied it of all my savings. What could I buy for five pennies? What could I *not* buy! I ran down the drive and another way round the great estate to avoid passing the gypsy encampment. I turned into the wood, hurried down the path to the pond.

I found no one. I could not call the girl. I had not learned her name. I sat by the pond, looked around again and again to see her come along the path. She did not come.

The afternoon was hot and still and silent of all but the pigeons calling high and away on the other side of the wood. Sitting by the still water made me still, emptied me of any wish for what was not about me. I forgot the gypsy girl. I took off my shoes and socks, stepped into the pond, stood there delighting in the cool squelch of the mud between my toes.

Suddenly the glass of the pond was shattered. A huge black snake broke surface only a little way from me; swirled, dived and disappeared.

I leapt back upon the grass bank, sat heavily down. Four great drops of blood fell on me. And laughter like rain. I looked up. The gypsy was lying along the low branch overhead. She threw down another fuschia flower. The breath left me in a great sigh.

'Ha!' the girl laughed. 'Frighted ye, didn't I?' She swung down from the branch. Her dress lifted as she dropped. I saw the flash of her nakedness. She landed beside me, grinning. 'Got t'other penny?'

I nodded, stood up, took a penny from my pocket, put it in her outstretched hand. I took another penny from the pocket, put it in her hand. Her eyes grew wider and wider as I put all the pennies I had, one by one, into her hand. Then I lifted out the linings of my pockets again.

'Five pennies!' The girl stared at the coins. Her hand closed over them. She looked at me, wondering what she could offer in exchange for so great a sum.

She took my hand and put it on the slight hill of her breast. A small tower stood upon it. Holding my hand there, she led me to the foot of the great tree nearby. She let go of my hand, lifted her dress, sat down among the exposed roots, spread her legs, then rolled up her dress, tucked it about her waist, leaned back against the tree, smiled 'Ye can look as long as you like now.'

I squatted before her. 'Ye can't see nothin' like that' she pointed out. 'Git down on yer belly.' I lay down on the grass. 'Come closer' she said. I crawled towards her, between the forked roots of her legs. I pressed down the grass. Sunlight fell through the leaves of the tree, dappled the ground before me, the thighs beside me. The earth smelled warm, live, animal. The pigeons' cooing increased the silence of the wood. 'Closer' whispered the girl. My cheek was now on her thigh. The split ripe fruit was not as smooth as I had first seen it; a bloom of red-gold hairs sprouted from it. I lay entranced.

After a while I looked up. The girl was smiling down on me in what I would come to recognise as the ancient ageless way of all women, young as old. The girl put the pennies on the ground beside her, said 'Stay,' while she drew up her knees, moved back upon her heels and squatted there, her thighs wide. With a hand on either side of the split she made an open wound of it. 'That's where babies come from.'

It was beyond all believing. The smallest babes I had seen were big as rabbits. This was at most a mouse-hole or, more alarmingly, a cranny from which a snake such as I had seen might come. But the girl said that humankind had exit there, there had entrance into the world. The girl was old and wise; she had not only secrets to tell, but also to show as part of her body and being. I must believe her. I lay on in wonder until the girl quietly asked 'Enough?'

It could never be enough, but I knew that I had had five pennies' worth. I nodded. The girl took her hands away, unhitched her skirt, stood up. I stood up beside her.

The girl said nothing. She put out her hand. I took it. She led me into the pond. I remembered the black snake but with my hand in hers went forward unhesitatingly, however fearfully. We went into the dark water up to our knees, laughed together, lifting our feet and putting them down again and again in the soft mud.

A shot rang out. Two pigeons clattered from the wood. The girl and I froze. The girl put a finger to her lips, turned about and pulled me from the pond. With her hand behind her holding mine, she went through the tall trees to the edge of the wide grassland bordering on the wood.

The girl went down on her knees and crawled towards the great house where the great Lord lived. I went down on my knees and followed. Some way into the open, the girl stopped and looked around. The land stretched away without sight or sound of anyone. The gypsy lay on her belly in the long grass. I lay on my belly beside her. The girl moved against me, smiled, then took up a grass stalk to chew. I did the same. The grass was sweet between my teeth and I could feel the length of the girl's body alongside, shoulder to thigh. I recalled what I had seen of her, making her a stranger, someone wholly *other* and yet, at my side now, not apart but a part of me: the difference she had revealed even brought us together, as two halves of a whole. I did not have such thoughts at the time, but lay glad and at ease as with some old and lost sense of Paradise miraculously regained at the side of the gypsy.

Like a true gypsy then, the girl took my hand, turned up its palm. Looking intently at it, she drew her ragged dirty nail down the centre of my hand — I would be rich, she said. (I could buy the sight of a *whole* gypsy, wholly unfrocked!). She put her nail between my thumb and forefinger and drew a curve down to the wrist — I would live long, she said. (With a stripped gypsy at my side!). Her nail crossed the top of my palm under the fingers to the base of the smallest one — 'You'll marry a Princess, most likely.' (A gypsy Princess in a yellow caravan, wearing golden earrings like crescent moons, necklaces of old silver coins, a red scarf, a swinging skirt).

I marvelled at her wisdom: how from a few faint lines on my palm she could so certainly foretell all the long course of my life. The girl put down my hand, stared across the great reaches of the estate. 'Ye'll live in a grand Lord's house like that, I shouldna wonder.'

I gazed at the likes of my future home and littered the tidy parkland with painted caravans; brought it to life with dogs and donkeys and naked children, wild-looking women and small men with great boots and checkered caps, barefoot girls in cotton dresses *and* out of them; the trees hung, the dark bushes emblazoned with coloured washing.

The door of the great house opened. 'Down!' cried the gypsy, her arm flung about me, pressing me to the ground. Slowly she lifted her head to look to the house. Slowly I did the same. A man came out: the Lord Himself! With his legs spread wide, he stood at the top of the wide flight of steps between the lofty pillars. He gazed around, a gun lying on his arm.

Then Himself started down the steps as though making for the girl and me. The girl clutched at my shoulder. Then Himself turned on the gravel drive and headed for some trees to one side. 'Maybe he's coming round the back of us' whispered the girl. 'We'd better git.'

We span about on our stomachs, got to our feet and, bending low, ran back into the shelter of the wood. There we straightened and ran on until we reached the lane on the far side. Breathing deeply there, we laughed together and aloud; the gypsy with her head thrown back, her arms widc. Then we were suddenly silent. We looked at one another, then turned and without a word took opposite directions: she to her tent, I to the house of the Priest.

As always, homemade soda-bread, yellow butter, thick cream, honey and strawberry jam loaded the tea-table, but I ate without appetite and refused the fruit-cake at the end. 'Feeling all right, boy?' asked the Priest. And then as I feared: 'What have you been doing all day?'

I hesitated a moment, then admitted that I had seen gypsies at the side of the lane. 'There was a horse and cart and a donkey and . . .'

'Tinkers' the Priest said. 'Not gypsies, *tinkers*. But they're much the same godless lot.'

I knew that I should not tell the Priest any more. *The Gods dwell above the navel* said the Greeks. I had looked below. I read the Greeks much later, but even at that time I could, with a child's compassion, understand that there were things one could not tell adults; even more that one should not tell teachers and preachers, things beyond the pale of their experience, beyond their ability to bear.

I changed the subject. 'I saw a snake.'

Again the Priest corrected me. 'There are no snakes in Ireland, Michael. I've told you that before.' He smiled, 'Saint Patrick saw to that!'

'It was in a pond.'

'Then it was an eel, boy, an *eel*.' If the occasion did not lend opportunity for a sermon, it allowed a short lesson. The Priest told of the habits of eels and of their habitat. When they were between five and eight years old (exactly my age!) the eels left the enclosure of their ponds and streams, the Priest said, and made their way to the Atlantic Ocean, then swam hundreds of miles to the Sargasso Sea.

'Yes! Yes!' I broke in. 'It's all thick seaweed and ships get stuck in it and rot and the sailors go mad and die and turn into skeletons and . . .'

'Stories!' said the Priest. 'Just stories, my boy. No truth in them at all.'

But the Priest could not bridle my imagination: Eels! The Atlantic Ocean! Storms and giant squids, blood-crazed sharks and heaving whales! The Sargasso! Shipwreck! Dead men! Skeletons! And there were great mysteries even among the bare facts that the Priest permitted. Eels might well swim down rivers and streams all the way to the sea and beyond, but if it was an eel that I had seen, how did it get out of the pond in the first place? Tell me *that,* I wanted to say.

But the lesson was over. The Priest wiped his mouth, folded his white linen serviette. His mind, gone from the ways of eels, was again given to his Book. I guessed that the Book was not about eels. The Priest pushed back his chair; without another word he went from the room. I heard the study door shut. The housekeeper also heard, and came to clear away the tea things.

'How do eels come out of ponds in the middle of fields and woods and find their way to the ocean, Mrs. O'Grady? How *can* they?'

Mrs. O'Grady laughed, 'You and your questions, Master Michael! Well, I'll tell ye: they come out at night in the blessing of the dark so's not to be seen, and the good Lord puts dew on the grass for them to slide over, the poor creatures. They sorta swim on the land, ye see. *That's* how.'

In bed that night, while waiting for the Priest to come up and supervise my prayers, I stared into the dark of the curtained room and reviewed all the bright day now ended. I conjured up the tinker's daughter whom *I* knew to be a gypsy. Had she not told me my fortune? I smelled the animal earth; against my cheek felt her thigh, soft and cool as the pillow now. I saw the strange fruit that the printed flowers of her dress ordinarily hid. I recalled her stare, her ancient smile, her gentle looking down on me. The wood-pigeons called again, called and called high and away on the edge of the wood. And the wood itself, in memory now even darker, was pierced by lances, by shafts, by pillars of light; and the pond, half gloom, half gold . . . the silence. Then the still water . . . the sudden swirl of the black eel . . .

I thought of that eel now, now that it was dark, sorta swimming on the God-given dew over the endless grass out of County Roscommon over high hills and hidden valleys to the saltwater of Galway Bay. The eel would stop a moment there, look up at the stars as every sailor of old to set his course, then take a deep breath, then swim out of the sheltering harbour across the wide and stormy wastes of the ocean towards the still haven of the Sargasso. . .

The landing light went on. It streamed under the door through a gap wide enough for an eel to squeeze through. I stiffened, pulled the covers up to my chin. But then I thought of the poor creature, starting on its long way, wanting to hide from the light of day, from the light that now streamed from the house onto the grass. The eel should come into the blessed dark of my room, hide under my bed until rested and reassured and ready to go on, with all the lights out and the grass under the night sky turned blessedly dark, black as himself. I let go the covers, smiled in welcome of the eel.

The door opened. The Priest entered, flicked on the light, sat down on the bed. I got out and knelt beside the bed. I could not understand the importance of such matters at the time, but the Priest was a Protestant only because his father was a Protestant. His heart all the while was in Rome, so that in addition to the Lord's Prayer I was taught to repeat *Hail Mary, full of grace* . . . and, *Holy Mary, Mother of God, pray for us sinners now and at the hour of our death* . . . It seemed right and reasonable to do so: as mother of the son of God, Mary was God's wife: to be given the same heed.

Nightly prayers apart, the Priest sometimes submitted me to Confession. I was in terror of such occasions because my sins never seemed sinful enough to satisfy the Priest, and clearly he did not believe that I could not remember more. Sometimes I would invent sins, as much for the Priest's sake as for my own.

This night of all nights, I had no need to invent anything. By the Priest's reckoning, I knew that I had had a devil of a day. This night of all nights, just as I had feared, the Priest decided it was time for Confession.

I lay silent.

'Well?' said the Priest. 'Well?'

'I . . . I saw some gypsies.'

'You told me that at teatime. And I told you that they were *tinkers,* not gypsies. Even if they are the same God-forsaken lot, there's no sin in seeing them.'

(Hail Mary, full of grace, don't let him ask me *what* I saw of one of them. Holy Mary, Mother of God, don't let him ask me that, please . . . *please.*')

My prayer was granted. The Priest said only, 'So you saw some tinkers. What else did you do?' He waited.

Desperate for sins, I remembered there were seven *deadly* ones. *Pride* was one. 'I climbed to the top of a tree, right to the top, and I felt *proud.*' The Priest was not impressed. He waited. *Gluttony* was another deadly sin. I confessed: 'I ate too much bread and butter for breakfast.' The Priest said nothing. He waited. '*And* marmalade,' I said. The Priest said nothing. 'Honey?' I added. The Priest remained silent, waiting upon yet deadlier sins. *Sloth* was another, but I could not even pretend to that; I had never been tempted to lie in bed of a morning. Another sin whose name I could not remember, had something to do with wanting over much. 'I wished I had more than sixpence a week pocket-money' I said. I did not say what for.

For want of a sin that gave off more smoke, the Priest settled for this. Sixpence, he insisted, was more than enough for a small boy. Children all over the world did not have enough rice to eat, let alone sixpence to spend. It only went on sweets and silly things, he added.

I looked as penitent as I could. I would keep my smile until I was again alone in the blessed dark.

After a small sermon, the Priest put his hands on my head in absolution. I said my prayers to God and His Wife. The Priest said goodnight, turned off the light, shut the door behind him.

I smiled. A tomcat yowled among the apple trees below. Was that the squeak of a bat? a vampire? Dracula? Everything was possible, was even likely. What had I not seen and heard and done that day! What might I not see, hear, and do the next day! Meanwhile I could sleep deep in the blessed dark with the eel curled under my bed, the frog on my pillow, the gypsy girl at my side, all the length and wonder and wild grace of her at my side, shoulder to thigh.

Unwittingly that day I had sided with the quick and the damned against the careful dead of the world. *Here* all about me were priests, and teachers, policemen and hunters and keepers with guns, all manner of respectable men with their churches, schools, prisons, zoos. *There* on the other side of the fence were eels, snakes, rabbits, mad march hares, foxes, badgers, tramps, small dark and great ginger women, lanky girls and gypsies. I was marked for life. Although I might assume the roles required by my elders and betters, I should be haunted always by the liveliness that seemed — for I was innocent as Ireland then — to belong to the lawless, to all who lived in the dark of woods or ragged beside lanes on the outskirts of great estates, out of reach — so long as they remained sly and lively — of men with guns, of God Himself.

I slipped out of the bed, went to the window, pulled the curtains, stared into the blackness below, then looked up at the sky, at the moon all of a mile away and the farther stars. I called: 'Who goes there?'

Then louder: 'Is *Anybody* there?'

I listened, waited.

'Well', I said at last, 'I don't *care.*' Like Kipling's Cat, I would walk by myself, waving my wild tail, walking by my wild lone. I went back to bed, pulled the covers up, slept deep, needing no dreams.

I leapt out of bed the next morning early and eager as always. Sleep on, everyone! I would say. Sleep, dream, snore and leave this First Morning to Brother Sun, to the last bat, to the first rabbit, to the fox, to this would-be wild boy, to the birds singing of that Great Silence before God gets up to thunder *Thou Shalt Not!* and men wake to echo Him, clouding the day with their commands.

But that morning I waited impatiently for all good men to waken and be about their lawful business, for prayers to be said, breakfast finished, and I freed at last for that lawless, godless gypsy.

At last Mrs. O'Grady came down, stoked the stove, boiled the kettle, brewed the tea, took it up to the Master. At long last, Himself came down. Prayers were read and blessings said while the world showed bright between my fingers. Breakfast was eaten in silence. I was glad for that. The Priest then went as every morning into his study to read his letters, look at the newspaper, get on with the Book. 'Be a good boy, mind you, Michael' he said on going. I walked slowly out of the front door and was a good boy all the way down the drive until I was behind the clump of rhododendron bushes and could be myself. I saw a group of lilies, thought of the girl, pulled one up by the roots. Loud as a morning star, I shouted for joy, and broke into a run. I ran along the lane around the great estate, around the wood until, with my chest heaving, I turned the corner towards the gypsy camp and the gypsy girl.

The girl was not there. No one was there. No one. Nothing. No dog. No donkey. No horse or cart. No tent. No man. No small dark woman nor big ginger one. No children at all. No girl. No girl at all. I walked slowly, unbelievingly. The downtrodden grass, the black circle of a dead fire, some litter, and a red rag waving from the hedge beyond was all that was left of my raggle-taggle gypsies-O.

I sat on the grass where the gypsies had sat. My lip trembled between my teeth, my eyes creased. Tears spilled. After a long while I lifted my head, sniffed, blew my nose on a dock-leaf, then got up to search for signs to show where the gypsies had gone. The tracks of the cart pointed to the way of the lane that went past the wood to join a road that reached over the hills to that secret valley where gypsies surely gathered to dance about midnight fires. I walked up the lane, started along the road a little . . . But the end seemed so endless.

A pigeon called from the wood. I turned back, ran into the wood in the wild hope to come upon the girl there, to call and conjure her up. But I lacked even a name by which to call her. The wood was as before — the fallen tree with its burst of orange fungus, the dark pond, the tall tree under which I had lain between the thighs of the gypsy. The exposed roots reminded me. The wood-pigeons reminded me, calling as always but in mockery now, *coo-coo, coo-coo.* The wood, the whole world was as before, but the light had gone from it, the girl had gone — without a trace, without a word, even without a name. I threw the limp white lily into the dark pond.

Out of the wood on the sunlit road again, I straightened, wiped my eyes, looked to the hills. The road reached away from me into the far-away and the future, disappeared behind a small rise, appeared, disappeared, appeared again, a long black snake over the green land winding into a haze of hills.

One day I would be a 'Man,' walking by my wild lone. Long-legged and free, I would follow that road over the hills through the haze to its end in the sunlit valley of dancing gypsies where I would again come upon that one and only girl.

I was, meanwhile, without any name by which to call her, summon her, address her in my dreams. I had no name for the wild girl until, many years after, I recognised her on the tower of the church at Rodel in the northern isle of Harris. Set in stone beneath a narrow leaded window, she squatted there as she had done since pre-Christian days, her thighs wide as a Bible open at *The Book of Revelations.* She was, I learned, to be found elsewhere in many sacred places, shameless and naked among the stone-robed saints — in the wall of the nunnery at Iona, squatting there over that window out of which virginal novices in spring may sometimes have looked, wondering on the world that they had left; where even older nuns sometimes, sometimes in autumn or in winter perhaps, may sometimes have sighed. The brazen lass was to be seen as a keystone in puritan priestly Ireland all the while that I was there, and is there to this day — *Sheela-na-gig,* Mother of the Dawn God, of the Sun Himself.

As *Sheela-na-gig* then, I held the gypsy in heart and mind. She was at the morning of the world for me; the lifting of her dress gave earliest hint of the bittersweet apple of awareness that would prove the death and the life of me. As the First Woman saw that the fruit of the Forbidden Tree was good, 'to be desired to make one wise,' and gave it to the Man at her side, so in her own small way that girl gave me sight, the possibility of insight. She was at the start of it all, the firstlight of love; the freckled, grimy, bruised and scratched, beguiling raggle-taggle Eve of my Beginning.

3 JANE

Girls that take off their clothes, and the naked truth
Have a quality in common.

Robinson Jeffers

STRIPPED, SHE STOOD WHITE AS A TUCK-SHOP PEPPERmint, her hands open and spread a little from her sides, *white,* but for one small part. After the black uniform she always wore, that sudden skin! the shock of her standing naked, the stare of her breasts, round as sunglasses, large as moons but full but soft but *seeing,* and in the treetop of her thighs that black nest, devil-black as pitch as night as that patch over the pirate's eye in the book by my bed, as catluck as blackbird as beautiful.

I was seven years old, staying on in a boarding school from which all the other boys had fled on holiday. Small as seven and alone, I roamed over playing fields that no longer played, climbed up trees and climbed down them, wandered in the gloom of a nearby wood, scribbled on a blackboard in a boyless classroom, walked the long corridor reading the names of absent friends above the hooks on which their grey coats, their coloured caps had hung. Only one cap now hung there, cerise and grey, with its rampant lion, its motto: *In Domine Confido.*

My trust in the Lord was severely tested. I had reservations about His stern representatives. For the most part of most days I hid from Him and from them in the long grass on the edges of the playing fields, or in the library where I could quickly escape to the Centre of the Earth, to Sherwood Forest, to the Wildest West, to the farthest

Poles, north and south. In all I read I sided with renegades, those on the wrong side of the fence about established law and order — Robin Hood, Big Chief Sitting Bull, Sir Galahad, St. Francis. When there was also a girl — a Maid Marian, or a Sister Claire — I was wholly involved. My own dreams sprang from such stories; each night before sleep I went to the aid of some damsel in distress, imprisoned in a high tower in Transylvania, or on an African plain backed against a tree in a ring and a roar of lions, or somewhere in the South Seas, Papete perhaps, or Murea, brown-skinned in a *pareo* of scarlet flowers or naked even, swimming in a lagoon whose blue calm water was cut, I saw, by the black fin of a shark.

Tales of chivalry and daring apart, I turned to comedy, taking heart from stories in which The Fool of All the World finally triumphed. Those who climbed mountains, fought raging fires, leapt chasms, flew through the air with the greatest of ease, seemed kin to those who hurled snowballs at tophats, dropped banana-skins in the path of bishops. All defied gravity. The Law of Gravity held me down; the Spirit of Levity lifted me. When the huge solemn Policemen chased the small grinning Clown, I ran with the latter.

The long day in that great house was interrupted by meals. On one bare table in the long dining-room one place was laid — one fork, one knife, a large and a little spoon. Crowding the walls were photographs dating back to the school's beginning: of cricket, football and boxing teams, triumphant with caps and blazers, silver cups and medals, swollen chests, but mute upon the walls now, poor company.

An Irish maid served my meals. She was just 'Jane,' plain Jane or, more plainly, 'the Maid.' Essential speech apart, no communication was allowed between female servants and gentlemanly schoolboys.

One day the Maid put a bowl of soup before me and broke the rule. 'It's a lonesome boy you are' she said. I looked down at the soup. The Maid left. She returned with beef, cabbage and potatoes. The Maid shook her head: 'It's not right — a little boy alone. 'Tis not right.' I dared to look up at her. In time the Maid brought rice pudding and smiled on me in the way of a Madonna once in a church in Connemarra. I wanted to weep for the small boy of whom she spoke.

At each long day's end, I went up the wide stairway from the lower corridor to the upper one, around a corner to a spiral of steps that led to a dormitory under the sloping roof. In the dormitory one narrow bed was made up, surrounded by the black iron frames and sagging metal springs of nine other beds. Against the rules, I often squeezed out of the small window and sat back upon the slope of the roof behind the low parapet that squared the house. A little to one side was another window; it was the Maid's room, I knew; and sometimes when it was lighted I wondered a little on her being there. I looked at the glow of the far-away town, at the dark of the night sky, at the slender and the swollen moon. Sometimes I saw a bat flutter or the ghost of an owl flap above the black trees. Sometimes the owl called *Who?* asked, *Who? Who?* I hurried back through the window, hurried into bed, pulled the cold sheet up to my chin.

At one day's end, I went slowly up the spiral of steps with a pile of books carefully balanced on my head, my arms wide as a tightrope-walker's. Janc the Maid came quickly up the stairs and, before I could move aside, gave me a small push. The books tumbled. Laughing, the Maid gathered them up, put them into my arms as I sat on a stair. The Maid sat down beside me, gazed at me with great seriousness a while, then smiled and whispered, 'Like to see my room, would you?'

I nodded.

'Get you ready for bed then and come.'

I leapt up the remaining stairs, ran into the dormitory, spilled the books onto the bed beside me, tore off my clothes, pulled on pyjamas, hurried round the corner to the Maid's room. It held a bed, lone and narrow as mine, a chair, a wardrobe, a chest of drawers. On top of this was a blue and white statuette of the Virgin Mary beside a framed photograph of a small white-washed cottage with a thatched roof and great stones on the end of ropes to hold it down. The cottage was surrounded by a low wall of larger stones. A stretch of calm water lay beyond. In front of the cottage stood a man, a woman, a boy, and Jane herself with a babe in her arms. 'My Ma, my Da, my brother boy, Sean' said the Maid.

I pointed to the babe in her arms. 'Who's that?'

'That's Pegeen' she said, picking up the largest of the several shells that lay about the photograph. 'Listen' she said, putting the shell to my ear. 'Hear the sea now? That's the way it is at home, just like that, mosta the time, with the wind roaring from the west.'

The sea and the wind roared on while the Maid went from my side. I put the shell down, picked up the others, one by one. The maid called from across the room, 'That big one I bought in a shop. The little ones I picked off the beach to remind me of home.' She added, 'You went to Ireland yourself now, didn't you?'

'Yes' I said and turned to her. She sat on the edge of her bed and was surprisingly pink; her shoulders and her arms were surprisingly white. The black uniform that had been *her,* lay on the bed together with the white starched collar and cap that had always sat upon her brow, held back her hair. Her hair was shaken free. Now she lifted up from the bed a little to peel off the pink petticoat. Now she stood up and, looking at me all the while, took the cloth from her breasts. Then, lifting one leg at a time, she took the last covering from her.

The Maid had taken only seconds to strip. I stood there many centuries while she did so. A long time had passed since the revelation of that gypsy in the wood, a whole year of schooling. Lessons and sermons had had their effect. I

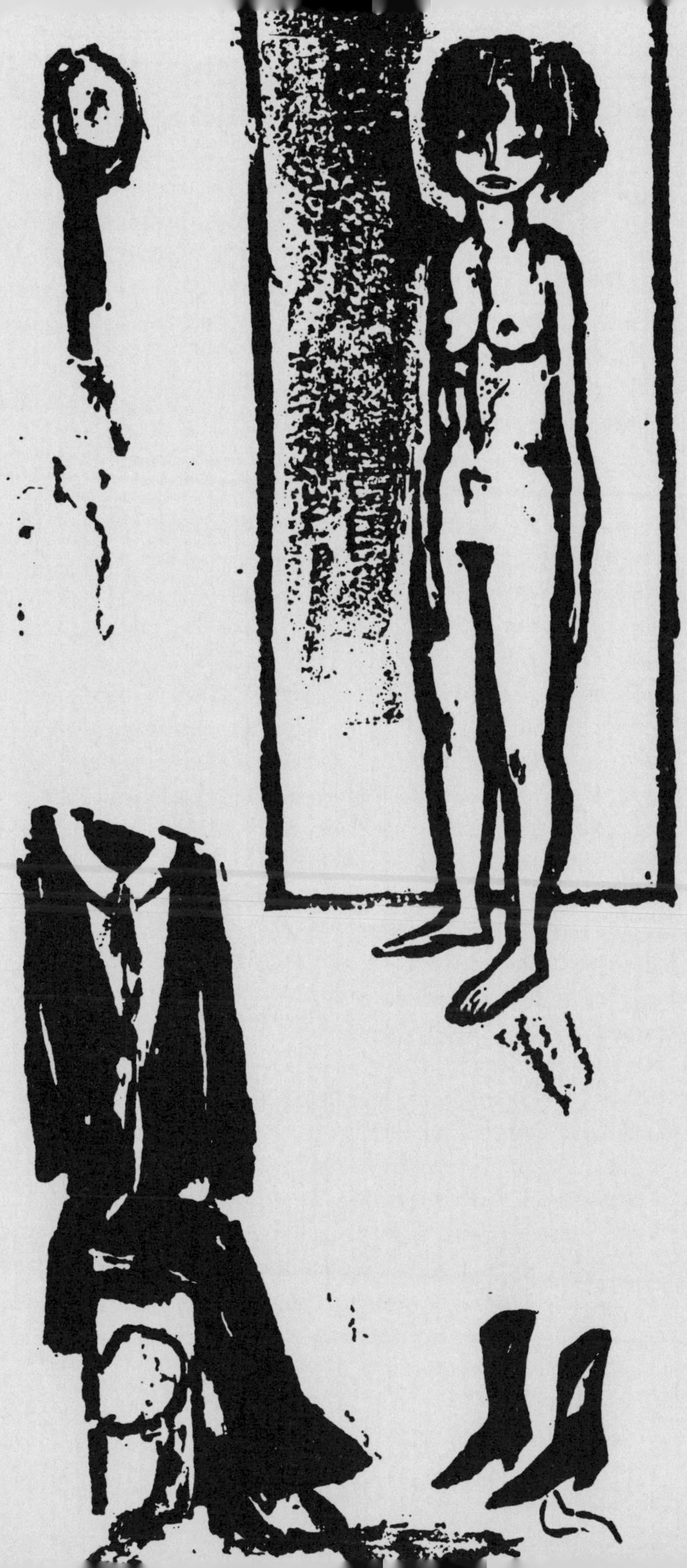

turned my back on the stark body, bit my lip, put my head to the door, stood trembling there, tears in my eyes.

The Maid who had stripped, it seems, to show the sad waste of her body to someone, to anyone, even to a seven-year-old schoolboy, now put on her nightdress and hurried to me, took hold of my trembling shoulders, turned me about, held me to her breasts, saying over and over, 'It's all right, Michael boyo. It's all right. It's all right. Nothing to be afraid of, nothing to mind, nothing at all.'

I pressed my face deeper into the shelter of her; fought back tears that were no longer fearful but from relief to be at a woman's breasts, to suffer their softness, all the old honey and new warm bread of the Maid's body; the woman smell of her; her arms about me.

I grew still. Gently the Maid pushed me from her, opened the door. She led me back to the dormitory, lifted the covers of the bed, helped me in, pulled up the blankets. 'Goodnight, boyo' she whispered. 'Go to sleep. Go to sleep now. Sure, everything's all right. Nothing to worry about. It's all right. I tell you. Go to sleep. Go to sleep now. Sweet dreams! God bless!' She bent over, kissed my cheek. As she lifted back and away from me, I could see, above the neck of her nightdress, her breasts swing back like heavy bells. She pushed the hair from my forehead, stroked my face, ruffled my hair, smiled, turned, went to the door. She called, 'Goodnight! God bless you, my fine boyo.' The door closed. I lay alone in the dark with the nine iron frames of nine empty beds.

I did not sleep. I stared at the dark of the ceiling; turned to the window and stared at the dark of the sky. Together with Latin and the Lord's Prayer, the school had taught me that it was a sin to see another boy naked. What had I done to see the whole white of a woman, and that black bit? I closed my eyes, only to see the full round and rose-centered breasts and, at the meeting of her thighs, that Sambo-black, shaggy pile. In spite of clenched fists and frightened prayers, my mind circled about, then stopped before that burning bush on the bare moorland of the Maid.

One week of the holidays remained. On the rare occasions when I happened upon Jane alone, it was *her* eyes that lowered. She said nothing. She went in fear, surely, that I would tell someone of that night of her nakedness.

The new term began. The long corridors filled again with jostling boys, shouting masters. I smiled: No one here, no one, not one knows what I know: that under her black uniform the Maid is white as a page of a new exercise book, but with an inky blot near its centre. And nobody knows but me — the Priest does not know, nor the Latin master, nor that of Maths nor even of Science knows what I know; not the Headmaster himself.

I never confessed her. I grew smug with my secret. In time I took strength from it. In time a sly smile passed between the Maid and me as she gathered up the greasy plates, piled them up against her soft breasts and told in her look her thanks for my silence.

Another term drew to its end. The excitement mounted over the last days. I joined in midnight feasts of sausage rolls, ginger beer, sweet cakes and toffees; shared in dreams and descriptions of homes in green fields, in wooded valleys, by golden beaches. In the eventual dark and silence of the dormitory I had to admit that they were, for me, only dreams.

No more pencils, no more books.
No more teacher's ugly looks.
No more things that bring us sorrow,
'cause we won't be here tomorrow!

I joined in the old rebel refrain on the last night. The last day dawned. After breakfast the other boys impatiently awaited the arrival of their parents, ran forward as the cars came, called goodbye to one another and to me, standing there at the start of the long gravel drive down which they disappeared. 'Goodbye!' I answered. 'Goodbye!' I waved. 'Goodbye . . . Goodbye . . .'

The last car with the last boy disappeared. The long drive looked lonely. I turned back into the empty house, went down the long corridor into a classroom — sudden, enormous silence all about me, within me. I put my head down upon a desk, dreamed of a small cottage in a snug valley somewhere with ropes and stones holding down the roof and a lighted window and my mother within and my father soon to return from the darkening hills. I wept a little at the way of things, at the 'tears of things' — a phrase I came upon later and at once understood. *Lacrimae rerum,* the Latin master called it. *Lacrimae rerum.*

I was in a classroom two days after when the Maid came. She had been looking for me everywhere, she said. She said she was leaving for Ireland. She wanted to say goodbye. She was not leaving for a short while only, not for a holiday, but for good. For *good?* My eyes filled. The Maid's eyes brimmed. 'It *has* to be, Michael boyo. I *hafta* go. That wee babe in the photo, remember? Pegeen — she *needs* me. She's mine. I'm her Ma. And there's no Da . . . I *hafta* go. You can see that. I *hafta* . . .'

She offered her hand. 'May the good Lord bless you, my fine boyo.' I took her hand and shook it like a 'Man', though I wished to be otherwise: to be a *very* small boy in the shelter of her breasts, the enfolding hills. 'Goodbye' I said. Unmanly tears were overwhelming me. For shame I turned from the Maid and ran out of the classroom down the long corridor out of the great house over the fields to an old friend, an oak that stood forty feet into the sky and as wide. I fell down in the shadowed grass, let the tears fall. My once warm secret was an old cold story now.

The tears dried. I turned over, lay on my back, looked up into the tree. I got up, ran and leapt up the great trunk to get a foothold, a hand on the lowest branch. High in the tree at a fork of two branches was a seat; an old dreaming place among squirrels, birds, beetles, ants for whom the tree was home. I had no home, not even a tree; not even the smallest cottage by the sea, with a roof secured against storms. At most I could remember staying places: a wagon, a railway carriage, rented places, flats in foreign cities, rooms in grand hotels. Now home was a great manor house, a school empty of all boys but one.

I closed my eyes: a boy in a tree dreaming of being a Man in the world one day when I would no longer need to dream: when I would open my eyes in a wood, in an attic, on a hill, in a garden somewhere, in Chimborazo or Cotopaxi or by Popocatapetl, anywhere, for all places would be alike to me then: and in every place Eve would be, in flesh and substance, naked, shining, her hands open and spread from her sides, spread wide, even reaching out for me, welcoming.

But it was another dream. Eve had gone from me to the far West of Ireland and for ever. Eve was not now. I could not hope that she would ever be. Again I was a boy alone, as always and always.

I bit my lip, looked through the leaves over the fields to the big house where there lived the headmaster, *Man* with his wife, *Woman,* and their huge Russian hound, *Dog;* to that *Cave* where — not being a squirrel, a bird, a beetle, an ant — I must go and live for a long while yet.

I climbed down from my dreaming place, sat on the lowest branch, hesitated, turned, slid down, swung from the branch, let go, dropped. After a moment with my face buried in the grass, I stood upright, took a deep breath, took one step with fear, took another breath; took another step with dread, another with daring, another with defiance, and another. *Man* might throw his boots, *as three proper Men out of five will . . .* and *Dog* might hunt me *as all proper dogs,* and *Woman* might say *Go away and walk by yourself in all places alike . . .* '[4] And I would do just that; not because She willed it, but because *I* was willing; because — for all the appearance of a small boy alone, of a small lonely boy, even of a small *lost* boy — I was in fact of all the Wild Things out of the Wild Wood, the Wildest; one of the great cats, even a *Lion* alone, and all places were alike to me.

I headed back to the big house walking by my wild lone, waving my wild tail.

The Irish Maid went from me to the west of Ireland for ever and ever and ever . . . yet remained within me, 'a light in the darkness.' I heard that phrase in chapel and turned it to my own purposes, invoking the vision of that Maid at the start of a race, in the boxing ring, as I dived from a high board into deep water or went reckless into a rugby scrum. I saw the shape of the Maid in clouds over the cricket pitch, in stains on the classroom wall. Sometimes in the midst of a lesson, of a scripture lesson even, she would come uncalled. Aware of her presence, I would stare at the blackboard to see only the white of her face, of her breasts, her wide white hips and the black of that bush, all the length and shining levels of her body and her hands spread wide, her dark eyes staring back. I would tremble and be glad, being no longer lonely, however alone.

Eden grew about me, radiant green in the dark of the dormitory at day's end. Eve came again, smooth and shaggy, naked out of Ireland. I had only to close my eyes to see

it was all
Shining, it was Adam and maiden.[5]

At twelve, I left that school for another of higher learning, to become better acquainted with the cunning of great Kings, the conniving of Popes, the cruelty of men everywhere. All wars were just, I learned, some even holy; the slaughter of innocents was necessary in the service of noble causes; the bodies of women and of men needed to be stretched upon the rack for their souls' sake; for the Good of all, unbelievers had to be burnt at the stake; for God's sake. I learned that Sister Water was two parts hydrogen, one part oxygen.

In spite of greater learning and growing experience of the world and its ways, an old innocence survived — and the vision of that stark naked Maid remained; the radiance did not dim; so that I stayed cool and easy (and ignorant) in spite of all the simmer and sometimes boil of an English public school. I put my fingers into my ears in the senior commonroom to muffle the derision of women, the gibes of those who so deeply, fearfully, guiltily desired girls, so hugely longed to know their nakedness. My desire was as theirs and as deep, but was for the most part without fear, without guilt. I had seen Eve naked and so could not be persuaded of evil. My friends dreamed brave deeds: of lifting skirts and downing trousers to see the little difference; dreamed one day or dark night of peeling the dress from some willing girl to taste the soft ripe fruit under. A little knowledge had been revealed to me in a dark wood once; even more in an attic. But I knew it would be misinterpreted, muddied over. Like Kipling's Cat, I told nobody.

I could not have told, for I could not have known at the time, how the nakedness of woman, *the work of God,*[6] had set my feet *in that part of life beyond which it is not possible to go with any intention of return.*[7] I could not have known that the gleam of that woman's body had brought a

> *dim and undetermin'd sense*
> *Of unknown modes of being.*[8]

4 ALICE

Oh, isn't life a terrible thing, thank God?
Dylan Thomas

WITH A MAN, A WOMAN AND A SMALL DOG IN IT, A car slowly wound its way up a high narrow road in Afghanistan. Around a bend at great speed suddenly: a lorry! The car swerved, skidded, slid over the cliffside, rolled over and over, faster and faster in a stream of rocks and stones . . . bounced, hit a boulder, stopped. The dust settled. The small dog pushed out of the wreckage, walked unsteadily a little way, ran.

I was ten years old when I heard the story. I was called out of an afternoon class to see the Headmaster. All eyes turned on me. What evil had I done? I made my way out of the main part of the house to the heavy door that led to the Headmaster's private quarters — entrance to the Head Monster's Cave, we called it. I went through. The door on its spring thudded behind me. A maid showed me into a room where the Headmaster and his mouse-like wife were waiting. They smiled on me, asked me to sit down. What good had I done?

The maid wheeled in a trolley with tea things. The Headmaster's wife poured tea, handed me a scalloped cup with small flowers on it, a matching plate. She offered me a cucumber sandwich, tiny and triangular, with the crusts cut off. What enormous good had I done?

After some generalities about the weather, about the cricket match to be played that Saturday, the Headmaster went on to speak of the 'game of life,' of not shrinking when the bowling was fast, of not giving up when the blows rained hard in the boxing ring; above all, of taking defeat with grace and of the necessity at all times of courage, at all times of being a 'Man.' The Headmaster asked if I had read Kipling's poem on the wall outside the library. I said I knew it by heart. The Headmaster smiled, 'And you understand it?'

'I think so, Sir.'

The Headmaster quoted:

If you can meet with Triumph and Disaster
And treat these two imposters just the same . . .

I told how I understood the lines. The Headmaster elaborated at greater length. His wife offered me buttered brown bread and strawberry jam. The Headmaster's sermon was a small price to pay. I looked as though I was interested. 'And how does it then go on?' asked the Headmaster.

I licked the jam from my lips, recited:

If you can make one heap of all your winnings
And risk it on one turn of pitch-and-toss
And lose, and start again at your beginnings
And never breathe a word about your loss;
If you can force your heart and nerve and sinew
To serve your turn long after they are gone
And so hold on when there is nothing in you
Except the Will which says to them: 'Hold on!'

The Headmaster beamed. 'Excellent, my boy!' His wife offered fruit cake. The Headmaster asked, 'And you understand what those words say?'

'I think so, Sir.'

The Headmaster ended the poem:

Yours is the Earth and everything that's in it,
And – what is more – you'll be a Man, my son!

What was it all in aid of? Had I been brought out of class for this? I did not wonder overmuch: the cake was good. His sermon over, the Headmaster cleared his throat. After a moment's hesitation and a glance at his wife, he started upon the story of the car in Afghanistan. I listened with more interest. Only at the end of the story did I realize that the man and the woman in the car were my father and my mother.

I did not cry. The deaths of my father and my mother were beyond imagining. But I could *see* the lorry come hurtling round the bend. I heard horns blow; brakes screech. I heard the woman scream. When the car at last came to a halt on the hillside, I saw a fender fly off; heard it clatter away. One wheel bounced on and on, fell on its side, slid, stopped. I saw the dust settle and the small dog walk away alive and glad to be. Wagging his tail? Where was that small dog now? I could see tears in the eyes of the Headmaster's wife. But the Headmaster was smiling. 'You're a brave boy, Adam.' He leaned forward and patted my shoulder. 'Your parents would be proud of you. So am I.' He rewarded me: I did not have to attend the last class of the day. It was Scripture, so that I was grateful. 'Thank you, Sir' I said.

I walked slowly from the room; walked faster through the heavy door that again slammed after me. The other boys were changing classrooms. Seeing me, they stopped.

'What did you do? What happened? Did you get a beating? How many? Did it hurt? How's your BTM?' They laughed and jostled me. I pushed my way through them, answered no one, said nothing, only repeated to myself: Hold on! Hold on! I walked as fast as I could through the crowding boys, then faster as the corridor opened up before me. I wrenched open the door at the end, ran out of the house across the gravel drive, over the endless fields to the long sheltering grass in the farthest corner under a crab apple tree. Only there, only then did I understand that my father and my mother were dead. Dead.

Quite soon, however, and forever after, my mind held only the image of a small boy lying in the long grass, uncontrollably sobbing. It was the memory of a fact; a sad fact but a past fact, simply a fact. What lived on was an image of the apple tree that hung over the boy. I seemed not to notice at the time, but the tree must have just broken into blossom, for the white and pink flowers on the green-leaved branches remained in memory, clear and bright against the dark wood beyond. Unaccountably, in the years after, it was not the memory of that sobbing boy, but the image of that radiant tree that moved me or, rather, made me still.

A cable from Sante Fe, New Mexico, announced the coming of Aunt Alice. She had seen me as a small child, but I had no memory of her. She was that unknown being who sent cards from all corners of the world: from Paris, Arles, Algiers, New York, San Francisco, Taos, Guadalahara, Mexico; even a view of Popocatapetl! Presents came too: a box of paints, red Moroccan slippers, a Mexican coin, a beaded Indian belt, an arrowhead from Texas and a real cowboy's knife with a blade that would take stones from my horse's hooves as I rode the wide range of wherever I was. The mystery of Aunt Alice grew with each gift and was increased by an awareness that the fondness with which my parents spoke of her was not without reservations. I heard my father laugh over a letter from Alice, 'She's crazy as ever!' I turned to see my mother's finger at her lips, bidding my father to silence in my presence.

Soon after the arrival of the cable, I was again shown into the Headmaster's room. A woman stood alone, looking out of the french windows over the lawn. She turned, but with the bright day behind, I could not see her face, only the dark enormity of her, ringed by light. She did not move. She gazed long and steadily at me; said nothing until she said simply, 'I'm Alice.'

I went to her. Disregarding the hand I stretched out, she put her great arms about me, held me to her. I had read of a 'bear's hug;' this was it. Alice drew back and held me at arm's length. Tears ran down her cheeks. She smiled, sniffed, let go of me, took a large red spotted handkerchief from the yellow striped bag that hung over her shoulder, wiped her eyes with it, blew her nose loudly into it, said 'Let's go, Michael. I'm taking you away for a long week-end at my cottage in Somerset, if you'd like that. Would you?'

I nodded. With my small hand in her large one, I went from the room out of the front door down the wide steps onto the drive. A tiny car was parked there. Alice squeezed into the driving seat. I got in beside her, excited by a sense of escape. Alice pushed off her shoes and with bare feet on the pedals, drove away.

For a long time nothing was said. When the roads turned into open country, Alice wound down the window, took deep breaths. Then she asked, 'Did you have a good cry?'

'A good cry?'

'Yes. When you heard about the accident.'

I hesitated.

'*I* cried' said Alice. 'I cried my heart out. They were so young, so much in love. They loved you so much and had such plans for you.'

'Yes' I admitted now, 'I cried *awfully*.'

'Good' said Alice. 'That's the way: have a good cry and then get on with your life. It'll get easier as time goes by, but I won't say that you'll get over it. How could you? Why should you? It's something you must live with. It's part of you, and a *good* part if you live with it. Everything lives and so everything dies — for Life's sake. Others die. We cry. And then get on with our lives — for Life's sake.'

These may not have been her exact words at the time, but that this was their meaning, I can believe from comments she was to make whenever death showed: as the tiny body of a wren in winter which I, with tears running down, held before Alice; as the dried corpse of a mouse that I found flattened against the wall by a chest pushed against it. There was dying but no death. There was no death *because* there was dying. The transformation of forms could not be called death since all were forms of the one

Life. This seemed to be her meaning.

I may not have understood at the time, but I was aware of something new in my life. In speaking of such grave matters with me, an adult had spoken without condescension. Alice might withhold thoughts that I was not yet ripe to receive, but she would not dissemble, she would not lie.

We started across Salisbury Plain with the sun going down before us. 'Soon you'll see Stonehenge' said Alice. She went on to tell of an ancient people nearly three thousand years ago bringing stones weighing four tons two hundred miles from the Welsh mountains; first floating them on rafts, then dragging them mile after mile over a rolling road of logs. 'But why? Why, Alice? Why? Why bring them all that way?'

'Because it was the *right kind* of stone and Stonehenge was the *only place,* the Sacred Place. There, with the aid of these stones in right arrangement, they could plot the rise of the sun and its setting, the movements of the moon, of the stars, and so plan the planting of their crops. It had to be that place on earth because of the way of the sky above.'

Alice brought the facts to light and life as none of the masters at school had done; she made a living link with the ancient races, made of the past a *presence,* here and now. I had only known lessons, the accumulation of dead facts. 'We've lost touch with the earth' said Alice. 'We're so *clever.* We know everything and nothing matters any more. We *feel* nothing. The little feeling that remains on earth is in the hearts of people whom we are pleased to call primitive, like the Red Indians.'

'Tell me about Red Indians, Alice.'

Alice told of those who roamed free, leaving no trace, no wound upon the earth; of others who settled like swallows in mud homes on high ledges of canyon sides; of those who, forced to make treaties with the White People, trusted them wholly, *for as long as the rivers will run and the grass will grow;* only to be betrayed, slaughtered, herded into reservations, their canyons flooded. Alice had tears in her eyes.

'Indians are always *bad* in cowboy stories.'

'Calling others bad is the way we avoid admitting how bad *we* are.' Alice went on to tell of the Indians' love of all creatures, of all things, of the earth itself; how they bowed to the tree before felling it, to the buffalo before hunting it; killing not for sport but for the survival of the same life in them as in the buffalo that lived by the death of grass. She told how things talked to Indians — hills, rivers, trees, the earth itself — how all things would talk to me if I *listened*. 'Did your school priest ever speak of Mother Earth? Did he pray to Her?'

I shook my head.

'That's because he does all his praying within four walls, shut off from the wind, from the sky and the earth. His God is at best a half-god, and so not God at all. The Indians speak of Mother Earth *and* Father Sky, both. 'Look!' she said, nodding to the sky ahead. 'There's an Indian chant:

Now Mother Earth and Father Sky
join one another . . .
And all is beautiful,
All is beautiful indeed.'

Alice stared at the great fire that blazed in the west: 'The Sky enters the Earth, makes love to Her and makes Her fertile. All creatures, all things come of their joining. Then the bright Sky falls asleep in the arms of Mother Earth who wraps Him about with darkness.'

I had read myths of many lands at school, but they were only stories. I had never heard such things seriously told. Alice spoke seriously, so that I felt in awe of all she told: of the Sky as it was here and now, of the Earth welling up with darkness, overwhelming the day.

'Stonehenge' said Alice. She pointed to a group of great stones against the horizon to the right. She turned off the road, stopped the car. In silence and last light, we walked over the grass with the stones rising higher and higher until we stood at the foot of one stone, enormous above us.

'Alice . . .'

'Sh! Not now. We can talk later. You can read about it later. But not now. *Feel* this place, its *presence.* The presence of these stones. Go off by yourself. And *listen* .

Nothing sounded on the earth. The sky hung silent over us, over all. Hesitantly I left Alice's side, wandered among the standing stones. I stood still now and then beside a stone, listening. I dared to touch one stone, to put hands upon it, then arms about it as far as I could, my brow pressed against it. The *presence* of things! I stood in awe but unafraid.

Night had flowed in and filled the spaces between the stones. I could not see Alice anywhere until I saw a solitary stone well outside the main circle. It called my name. Alice and I got into the car, drove on into the night.

Nothing more was said about Stonehenge. I had more questions but they could come later as Alice had said. Instead I asked, 'Do you believe in Heaven, Alice?'

'You mean some other place where someday you'll meet your father and mother?'

'That's what Mr. Sincock, the school priest, told me.'

Alice was silent a while. She whispered 'Who knows?' Then with more spirit, 'But *no,* Michael, I don't believe it. There's no Heaven and no need of one. No hereafter. And no need. Whatever happens, happens *now.* Whatever *is,* is here. Your father and mother are dead. You'll not see them again, but don't you *feel* them, here and now? And I don't mean just remember them.'

Did Alice speak of ghosts? It was dark outside. I pressed back and down into the seat. After a while I fell asleep.

Alice woke me on arrival at her cottage. I went, with her help, to bed. She kissed me and left me lying there with moonlight flooding the room. I looked back over the day, remembered the great stones, the bright of the sky and the earth in darkness; all the many things Alice had told. Suddenly I was overwhelmed by awareness of my parents, of their presence. Tears ran down as they had not done since that day in secret under the crab apple tree. Yet my sadness was not apart from a glad awareness of my father and my mother within me, with me now in some strange but certain way. And gladness here and now to have Alice with me in her most substantial way: the warm enormous bulk of her at back of me, beside me in the world now and forever: *as long as the rivers will run and the grass will grow.*

Early next morning I opened my eyes on a strange room. I got out of bed, went to the window, gazed on a strange world, misted, still moonlit. After a while a cock crowed. A long silence followed. An owl hooted.

And then, small as the start of a heath fire, like the first leaks of a bursting dam, like nothing in all the world but the beginning of a May morning in England, a few wayward phrases of song started among the blossoms of an apple tree. A blackbird began it, then a thrush joined in, then a tit, a robin, a finch, a wren, a cuckoo, and soon, soon all England's birds had joined in one chorus of warbles and whistles, trills and cheeps and ringing calls of far-away pigeons and nearby cuckoo — sounds of air and water, even of the underworld, as the hoot of the owl; all increasing and unceasing until, quite suddenly, it slowed, subsided, stopped. A few stray notes fell. A starling whistled. Some sparrows twittered. Then silence. The moon had greyed, had now gone. The mist lifted. The white of a hawthorn showed. A heron rose out of the valley. Slowly, silently, on great grey wings, it flapped out of sight. Without a sound the sun came up.

The front garden was now alight. Within the square surround of a high box hedge, I saw smaller gardens, patches of grass, roughly circular and surrounded by low bushes and flowering shrubs, all linked by a winding path. I turned from the window to dress and hurry down, but was slowed by all I could see in the room. Above the bed three Red Indians stared back at me: a fierce old man with a hooked nose, a squaw with the face of a dried walnut; between them a small boy astride a great white horse on an immense plain reaching back and beyond. On another wall hung a bright Navajo weaving, a dark African mask, the painting of a bird with black eyes peering out of an emerald bush of impossible beauty. Necklaces of beads and coloured stones hung from old nails. By the door a crucifix of two pieces of driftwood bore a stark naked Christ, smiling, with immense eyes, with widespread arms.

But I was eager to be out. I dressed and hurried past all the other treasures that the landing showed, and those that lined the staircase. I went into the kitchen with its red stove and open shelves of coloured pots and plates and cast-iron pans, out of the front door into the garden. Soon I heard the front door open. Alice came, from neck to ankle in a woven robe with strange marks on it; on her feet red Moroccan slippers of the kind she had once sent me. I watched through a hedge as she raised her arms and spread them wide, the sun full upon her. Some Red Indian ritual? Salutation to the Rising Sun?

I did not move. Alice went back into the house, to reappear with breadcrumbs and seeds for the birds that gathered about her. She called 'Johnjohn.' A blackbird with one leg flew down to her feet. A robin fed from her hand. Other birds came. She spoke familiarly to one and all.

I went to her. 'Ah, Michael! So you're an early bird too!' She embraced me. A duck and a drake waddled towards her. 'That's *Para'* she said, pointing to the drake, and to the duck, 'That's *Dox.* This is Michael' she told all the birds. 'He's come to live with us.'

I smiled. I assumed she was playing a game. So she was. But I would learn that she was all the while in earnest: birds, beasts, rocks, bushes, flowers of all kinds, weeds and vegetables were alive for her as much as humankind, all having consciousness of varying kinds and measures. Unashamedly animistic, she greeted all in her garden as she had greeted me. She put a hand fondly on a flowering plum tree as on my shoulder to lead me back into the house for breakfast.

I went back to school in a daze of happiness. At the end of the term I waited on the drive with the other boys; in time, in my turn, I got into the car that was to take me home. I looked over my shoulder to the space where a boy had once stood, small and disconsolate.

From that time on, I went each holiday to the cob cottage that Alice shared with the ghost of a girl who had been slighted by her lover three centuries before and had hung herself from the bacon hook in the blackened oak beam of the kitchen. 'It's Elizabeth' said Alice simply, fondly, whenever the night unaccountably creaked. That old hook now dangled the string of onions brought on a bicycle each month by a Breton in a beret. Alice was a vegetarian. She planted her lettuces by the light of the waxing moon, had herbs for every ailment, balm for every wound. When I fell out of the copper beech, she bound my leg with comfrey leaves.

Alice was *very* vegetarian. Visited by an old friend, an earnest Buddhist and Theosophist (Alice had been both in her time, and as earnestly), Alice made a salad in a large wooden bowl; to it was added not only nasturtium leaves but also the red flowers, to be eaten. Dark bread of her own baking came with it, cottage cheese of her own making, nuts and raisins. On a separate plate lay slices of ham, specially brought for the occasion. To my surprise and to the horror of her high-principled friend, Alice ate a slice of ham with apparent relish. When the friend had gone, Alice, her nose wrinkled with distaste, threw the rest of the ham away.

The inconsistency of Alice made her whole. With strong opinions on every subject, she had no respect for opinions. 'All opinions are poppycock' she said; then smiled and added, 'In my opinion.'

Her poor opinion of Christianity did not square with her habit of singing Christian hymns when she painted; nor with her vast collection of crucifixes from France, Africa, Mexico and elsewhere. Some, made and painted by Alice, could be recognized by the Christ they held. While the other crucifixes supported a figure heavy with sorrow and a sad head, Alice's face of Christ was that of a Sun God, radiant and serene. One painting showed Christ wholly at ease upon the cross, his head held high; his right hand dangling the mask of tragedy, his left hand the mask of comedy. Midway between them large eyes stared back at the beholder; the mouth lit by a half-smile suggested some secret joy. Saints and angels were also frequent in her paintings, but they seemed always a little in league with the Devil, up to some divine mischief.

Alice's scorn for priests and schoolteachers in general never extended to a particular priest or teacher. The local vicar was a good friend and frequent visitor. Invariably they entered into lively argument. Alice would demand of him again and again: 'How *can* you believe such rubbish? a grown man like you, a *bright* man?' The vicar, a most gentle gentleman, smiled not only in the certainty of his own faith, but as much out of the conviction that Alice's expressed views and protestations were only pretence. 'Her whole way of life belies her stated beliefs, and her unbeliefs' he told me later. 'She's more of a Christian than anyone else in the parish.' He added, 'I include myself.'

'The whole way of life' of which the vicar spoke was surely the womankindliness of Alice, the open arms with which she welcomed all and everything, including the sadness that visited her sometimes, and the occasional sickness which, she said, was welcome evidence of the body healing itself; all one needed to do was fast, drink water, wait. Though it was not in the prescription she gave me, she often sang hymns at such times.

Alice had wide arms for everyone — young people in the trouble of love, older people in lack of it; lame dogs, sparrows brought down by small boys with guns, and small boys with guns whom she fed with stern words and chocolate cake. She supported every cause for the alleviation of distress, for the benefit of prisoners, of beaten children *and* of those who beat them; of pit ponies, old donkeys, badgers, otters, whales and seals. She fumed at the sight of fur coats, at bright feathers gracing the hats of church-goers on their way to praise the God of all creatures great and small. For love of animals, she opposed both hunting and household pets. She never picked wildflowers. Saddened by the sight of daffodils picked and then left by the roadside, she lifted them up, put them gently into a stream, watched them out of sight. She never picked wildflowers but, visiting a sick child, she searched for early violets and bound them in a posy. Alice willingly admitted to being 'soft.' She was not sentimental. Tears ran down as she freed and lifted a small rabbit mangled by a trap; she spoke gently to it, cradled it in her great hands, caressed it. Then she cracked its neck.

Not only live things had Alice's attention and love. She spoke to her kettle, to her pots and pans, as some will converse with cats. She spoke sternly to her stove when it failed to respond, patted it when it did. She held her teacup in two hands as one might a chalice, gazing at it before drinking from it. She saw all bread out of her oven as consecrated, passed her hand over a chairback or a table as another woman might caress a man.

There was no man. Alice's ability to love was great as her body, but that body had been in the way. She was enormous and unlovely. Lacking a man to embrace, she had embraced that lack and, by the alchemy of things, her loneliness had been transformed into an aloneness that allowed her to delight in love and all its manifestations. She was without envy.

She had told me that the Sky 'made love' to the Earth. I was to hear that the newborn calf in a nearby field came of a bull's making love to a cow; the stallion I saw mount a mare was making love; so was a gull on another gull's back; so were two dragonflies joined in flight over a stream. Men and women, I learned from Alice, made love in the same way, in what the theologians called 'the manner of beasts,' with the added possibility of a transforming awareness of what they did. 'Bestial' was not a term of abuse in Alice's mouth. She was no theologian.

Happily then, it was with Alice that I first saw a man upon a woman. We had turned off a high path on the moor to stand on the edge of a combe in the hope of seeing deer below. I saw a man in the bracken, with his trousers down upon his ankles, at length upon a woman with her skirt drawn up. He seemed to be stabbing her. Alarmed, I whispered, 'Look, Alice, he's *killing* her.'

'No' said Alice quietly, 'he's not killing her.'

'He's *hurting* her.'

'A little. But I doubt that she minds.'

Her point was proved. The man made a last lunge, then lay still upon the woman. Her naked legs now lifted, crossed over and held the man to her, her hands ran over his back. 'Come' said Alice. 'We mustn't spy on them.'

'But what were they doing, Alice? What were they doing?'

'They were making love' she said. I saw tears in her eyes, so that I could not ask the next question: What did it mean — 'making love'? Was it something I too would do when I was a Man? Would I stamp the ground and snort like a stallion, steam coming from my nostrils? Or like the gull, would I clamber onto the back of a girl who would lower to the earth under me and I would beat my arms in the air and cry out and cry out? Or in Horner Wood or Timberscombe would I take down my trousers and with my body stab a girl and she would be glad of it somehow? and would she then embrace and enfold me as the Earth itself received the Sun, then wrap me about with darkness? Was love some fate awaiting me? With manhood and the coming of love would I be seized each spring as every other creature, be lifted up and hurled down, be *made* to make love? I walked silently at Alice's side, knowing that I could ask no more of her at that time. I could not ask why there were tears on her cheeks.

I learned of this later when the growing awareness of my own body made me eager to know more of love. I wondered about Alice: she spoke of love so lovingly, yet there was no man in her life as far as I knew; nor had ever been.

'Ha! You mean I'm an ugly duckling? an ugly duck? a toad? No man could love me?' Alice grinned, 'Is that what you mean?'

Before I could protest, she went on, 'You're right. I *am* a toad, though that's unfair to toads.' She was a long while silent. Then she said, 'But yes, Michael. I *have* loved a man. And believe it or not, he loved *me.* At least he made love to me often and in the strangest places.' She chuckled. 'He said he loved me. At any rate he *appreciated* me. He was a painter, you see, and for a painter nothing is ugly; a painter sees things simply as they are — toads, ducks, apes, elephants, *me.*'

Her eyes clouded over. I waited. Staring into the fire, Alice then told me that she had given up her work as a designer for a weaving firm out of the want to be a painter. She went to Paris. At the atelier where she went to draw from the live model, she met another young painter, small and very thin. 'He complained that the models were too much like himself. He wanted *mass.* He said that I was the fulfilment of his dreams, the model he sought. My body was firmer then, not so shapeless, though it was big. I went that afternoon to his attic and stripped for him. He worked at great speed in brightest colours, with huge blobs of paint worked with large brushes, with a knife, with his fists, his fingers, crying out from time to time, groaning sometimes like a woman in labour. After three hours he was exhausted. He came to the couch on which I lay, fell into my arms, slept on me. When he woke, he made love. He made love to me that day and that night and every day and night until he went away.'

'Went away?'

'Was *taken* away . . . The war,' she explained. 'The

madness. He never came back.' She stared into the fire a long while. Then she said 'I haven't loved a man since.' She added with a grin, 'Not many men have Gaston's great appetite.'

Gaston! I could now decipher the flourish in the corner of that huge canvas in Alice's bedroom. The figure stood stark and central on a ground of gold, like a detail from a crucifixion, cut off at the neck, above the elbows, above the knees — a woman's body, quite narrow at the shoulders, but swelling enormously at the hips — all in shades of red, with great breasts and nipples like purple grapes, dull golden tufts of hair under the armpits, a fiery golden bush below the belly, laid on with firm loving fingers. 'That painting in your bedroom, Alice?'

'Yes, that was me, painted by Gaston in the last summer before Armageddon.'

Alice never spoke again of this one man in her life, but I was reminded when I borrowed a book of poems from her shelves. One passage was heavily underlined:

My Dear One is mine as mirrors are lonely,
As the poor and sad are real to the good king,
And the high green hill sits always by the sea.[9]

In pencil, in the margin was the cry: *G! G!* I read the lines over and over without understanding, but their mood was clear. I sensed why, that day when we had looked down on the lovers in the combe, Alice's eyes had filled with tears.

Alice's entry into my life was the start of my real education. To all I learned in classroom and in chapel, she opposed the heresy of happiness. Joy was the mark of goodness, she said, and a grim man was therefore less than good. I could now shed my awe of teachers and preachers, my fear of wrong-doing. 'Dare to make mistakes, Michael. How else will you learn except by suffering your mistakes, by licking your wounds?' But suffering was no virtue, Alice insisted; it was not to be ennobled since it was evidence of error. Err, and so naturally suffer the consequences; then seeing the error, have done with it, forget it, do otherwise, begin again. And again. 'Thinking about sin *is* sin' she said.

Alice's attitude ran counter to all my upbringing. She approved my bastardly beginning. 'Lucky boy, you were a love-child,' she once said. She praised the early lives of my mother and my father, but regretted the respectability they later sought, and sought for me. She did not approve my schooling, but carried out my parent's plans. I went from a preparatory school to a public school as they had wished. School was a dark tunnel through which I must go. Alice did her best to lighten it. She sent me quotes and books by Whitman, Thoreau, Lawrence, Yeats, Rimbaud, so that in secret I stroked my beard and pondered *night, sleep, death and the stars.*[10] I played a flute in a drifting boat on Walden Pond. While planting nine bean-rows in a bee-loud glade, I planned a *long, immense and reasoned derangement of the senses, all forms of love, of suffering, of madness . . . to be a Stealer of Fire.*[11] Invited to have tea with the Housemaster and his wife one afternoon, that night I stole the wife away and set off from Charing Cross for the Isartal and over the Alps to Sicily:

And so I cross into another world
shyly and in homage linger for an invitation
from this unknown that I would trespass on.[12]

I dared it all under the guise of an obedient schoolboy. That I was 'inclined to dreams' was about the worst that my masters reported of me. *What demon possessed me that I behaved so well?*[13]

In the holidays, I would find about the house postcards with texts taken from Alice's wide reading. They would remain for some days, sometimes for weeks, propped on the mantlepiece or pinned to a door, taped to a wall. They disappeared, to be replaced by others. Many that were beyond my understanding at the time remained in memory to reveal their meaning later: often while I was licking my wounds.

I was about twelve when I saw, pinned to the toilet door, the question:

What rough beast, it's hour come round at last,
Slouches towards Bethlehem to be born?[14]

Once, going there at night, I left the light off and stood very still with the strange words there in the dark. Then I hurried to open the door, ran back to bed. That verse was in time replaced by another:

Lady, if the dirt should gleam,
Feel, but do not show surprise.
Things that happen here would seem
Paradox in Paradise.[15]

'What exactly does *paradox* mean?'

'Exactly?' Alice smiled, then said, 'Let's look it up.' I went to the Oxford Dictionary. I read out: *A statement or tenet contrary to received opinion or belief . . . seemingly self-contradictory or absurd, though possibly well-founded or essentially true . . . often applied to a proposition that is actually self-contradictory, and so essentially absurd or false.*

'It seems to say that a paradox can be both true *and* false.'

'Of course: it's paradoxical.'

I did not understand.

'It's not to be understood, Michael. Someday you'll *see* it.'

'You call your drake *Para* and your duck *Dox*. Why?'

'Because that's their names' said Alice. '*And* their nature. Aren't they absurd, as the dictionary says? And aren't they true? But dictionaries can only offer more words. They can't make you *see*.'

Para and *Dox* could be seen out of the window. I could not see their absurdity; the fact of them, but no more. I said so.

'You're *trying* to see' said Alice. 'That way you'll never see.'

Some weeks later when Alice and I were in the garden, Para waddled purposefully towards Dox. After a brief discussion, Dox lowered to the ground. Para mounted her. Alice caught my arm, pointed, 'See, Michael: *Paradox!*'

I saw all that went on at the time, but many years were to

pass, many wounds needed to be licked before I saw her point.

Alice's paintings hung about the house. They were for the most part of recognizable creatures and corners of her garden. Four great sunflowers grew one summer near the back door, and grew again on a tall narrow plank of wood that stood in the hall; a one-legged blackbird at the bottom stared out from the green stems. Another plank, as long and narrow but hung horizontally, showed a full moon risen over the garden hedge at the foot of which a rat sat with the same staring eyes. A frog with its eyes above the surface of her small pond regarded one with the same steady look. These large staring eyes in so many of Alice's paintings were perhaps a reflection of moments when she herself stood, was still, and *saw*.

Above all, it was her Paradise paintings that revealed the essential Alice. All the years of my growing up and my growing down, I saw Alice as a rock in a stream, as a spreading oak; a woman who, for all gentleness, was stronger than any man I knew. These paintings suggested the source of that strength — a humility and hesitancy in the light of some larger Life than her body could contain, her own strong being command.

The main figures in these paintings were the same: God was in them, a small plump, bushily-bearded man in a tweed suit. Adam in them was a little taller, very thin, with a whispy beard. He looked, I realized, as a French art student *should* look. Eve was of the build of an ancient Mother Goddess, with narrow shoulders, broad hips, a great golden mane of hair about her head and shoulders. The Garden was essentially that garden on which Alice looked down from the room where she painted, but it was circular and in the centre of the canvas, within the square of the box-hedge that enclosed her own garden and ran as a frame around these pictures. The central Garden, in contrast to that surrounding it, was lit by extraordinary light. The Garden was walled; in the wall was a small door.

Alice's interpretations of Genesis were unorthodox. In one painting, God with one stern finger raised, was warning Adam and Eve not to eat of the fruit of the Tree of Knowledge, while his other hand behind his back was passing the Apple to the Serpent, who was clearly a collaborator. In another painting, the Serpent was even more — he lay at the foot of the Tree with the bearded face of God Himself; a sly smile on his lips, one eye glaring at the beholder, the other closed in a wink. Alice explained: Nietzsche had told how God, at the end of his great work of Creation, had curled himself up at the foot of the Tree in the guise of the Serpent.

In three of these paintings, in the shadowed area surrounding the walled Garden, was a Woman of the size and shape of the great Eve within, but robed, with red Moroccan slippers on her feet. In one painting, this woman sat astride a branch of Alice's copper-beech tree that reached far over the wall of the inner Garden. The branch was bending under the Woman's weight and was split where it met the main trunk. I pointed to it. 'The branch will break. She'll fall.'

'It is to be hoped so' said Alice.

Another of these paintings showed the old chest that

stood in Alice's drawing room with two hearts carved on it and the year 1737; here it was on the grass outside the curved wall of the Garden; on it stood the high stool on which Alice sat while painting; on this was a bright Mexican bean-pot taken from the kitchen. On tip-toe at the top of this precarious tower was the same Woman, recognizable by her red slippers and by the broad bottom that showed this side of the wall while the rest of her leaned far over, looking into the confines of Paradise.

The last of the paintings showed the Woman standing before the small door in the wall around the Garden. The door was open and the light of the Garden streamed out, enveloping the dark figure of the Woman with a bright sheath, an aureole. 'Look! Look!' I said. 'The door is open! She can go in!'

'The door is never locked' said Alice. She pointed: 'But see the bulk of her. And look at the narrowness of the door.' She laughed. I wanted to weep.

One painting by Alice owed its origin to me. Much of my summer holiday was spent wandering alone over Exmoor. With the growing wants of my body and the increasing awareness of womankind, I found correspondence in that landscape. On my return home one day, I scribbled notes of *hipped and breasted hills . . . the thigh of a ridge . . . hollows with bushes of pubic hair . . . deep female combes and caves.* I left the scrap of paper somewhere.

Little was seen of Alice over the next two days, but I heard her singing low and slowly over and over:

Abide with me.
Fast falls the eventide,
The darkness deepens,
Lord with me abide . . .

I knew she was painting. I returned to my room after another long walk on the second evening. Beside my bed hung a moorland landscape that was all the while a woman lying down. 'Did you know' said Alice, 'that the Navajo Indians speak of the earth as *The Recumbent Woman?*'

She went on to say how true had been my feeling for the earth as woman; how it had been the way of all ancient peoples whose understanding had not withdrawn into their heads. Most of the Old Testament may be forgotten, said Alice, but I should again read *The Song of Songs*: the 'garden enclosed' was the womb of woman; the 'gate' was the vulva.

I walked on the moor with renewed wonder. I found a solitary place, stripped to the sun and lay upon the earth to read:

Within the curcuit of this ivorie pale
Ile be a parke, and thou shalt be my deere:
Feed where thou wilt, on mountain and in dale,
Graze on my lips, and if those hils be drie,
Stray lower, where the pleasant fountains lie.

Lying naked on the moor, reading and dreaming under the sun of that long summer, I grew browner but no less bewildered, having no girl under me. I had never known the wild garden of any girl, so that it was not a lost Paradise for which I longed. I wanted nothing mythical, nothing metaphysical; no future at the side of God the Father, no past in the lap of a Mother Goddess. I had long accepted my orphan state and had no want of parents; my need was nuptial and was *now:* the wish simply for a girl at my side, human, fragile, fallible as me; at my side in the world as it was, all the crippled wonder of it, just as it was.

I looked on the swell and the shine of the summer moor, then closed my eyes in the certainty that Eden was all about me even then, if only I could *see.* I was barred from the Garden, being innocent beyond my time. I was ignorant and so was blind. I remembered the old words: *She took of the fruit of the tree thereof, and did eat, and gave also unto her husband with her, and he did eat. And the eyes of them both were opened.* Without the gift of that apple from the hands of a girl, without the fruit of that forbidden tree, I could not grow up, could not be a 'Man,' could not begin to live, could not see, could not *be.*

Eden was not at the junction of two rivers in a far-away land of long ago; it was at the meeting of a girl's thighs and so was here if *she* was here, if she would lie back upon the earth, stripped, wide, welcoming. I would enter, and in coming upon love I would come upon the world, the flesh, *and* the devil if need be. Gone beyond blind, fearful obedience, I would take that apple gladly, unwithholdingly, wholly, all the sweet and sour of it. As now, as always perhaps, I would walk by my wild lone but, by way of woman, in the bittersweet world at last.

I dreamed long and dreamed well. But then I opened my eyes, saw that I was alone. Under me was only the body of the moor. I put my head down on it and, for lack of a girl's hair, clutched at the grass.

5 ANON.

. . . Love, half angel and half bird
And all a wonder and a wild desire.
Robert Browning

DREAMING IN THOSE DAYS, IN THOSE NIGHTS, OF the coming of love, I would see landscapes: a green hill, a wide clear sky, a sun; I would hear larks. In a darker mood, I would see a shadowed wood, hear rooks croaking in the high branches.

Once, in such a wood my eyes had been opened by a girl who had lifted her skirt and squatted among the exposed roots of a tree while I lay entranced on the earth before her. And although it was in an attic that I first saw a woman wholly naked, my mind in time made a landscape of her body; finding support among the poets, even in the Bible: *Thy belly is as a heap of wheat set about with lillies . . . Thou art a fountain of gardens, a well of living waters, and flowing streams from Lebanon.*[16]

I had seen my first lovers in a sunlit bed of bracken in a deep moorland combe. And later, in a Kentish field in the summer evening shadow of a line of hop poles wreathed with green and starred with male and female flowers, with a thrush calling somewhere, another woman in my sight, another man, teased one another, wrestled and laughed, then were suddenly serious, then were still, then silent. The woman's knees yawned to receive the man.

I could not imagine any girl without her green setting.

One girl lived in memory as part of a hawthorn hedge with its wild grasses, beetles, birds' nests, bramble, dog rose and bryony.

A yellowhammer had called beside the dusty path, but when I stopped and sat down on the edge of a field of yellowing wheat, I heard no sound of the bird, and had no sight of any other. Summer noon had silenced all, sent every creature into the shade, emptied the world of everyone but a lizard lazy on a stone. I stripped, lay back against the hedge, closed my eyes, slept.

I woke, surprised by singing; not a bird's but a girl's voice, growing louder. I hurried to pull on my trousers, then realized that the girl was on the other side of the thick hedge and would not see me if I was still. I was still. I peered through the hedge, saw the flickering patches of her dress as she passed close by and, singing all the while, went beyond. Then I no longer heard her and supposed she had walked on and away. I settled back against the hedge with an early apple and *The Canterbury Tales.*

I was into another apple and 'The Miller's Tale' when I heard a small cry. I put down the book, crept along the hedge until the yellow of the girl's dress showed on the other side. I tried to make a spy-hole but the thorns tore at my hand. I drew back and had to be content with the sight of small fragments of the girl's dress, much the same colour as the flowers of bryony.

From the pattern of the yellow patches, I knew the girl lay in the grass. After that first cry she made no sound, but she was not lying still. I could see the lift, shift and dance of her dress, could hear her breathing — short, deep breaths, let out in deep sighs that turned to moans, to groans. Was she sick? Dying? But the dance of the yellow patches grew more lively and the girl cried aloud, 'Oh! Oh!' then 'Ah!' then 'Darling, darling, *darling*', over and over, faster and faster, her voice rising higher and her dress leaping, until a long last cry, *'Agh!'* The yellow dress shuddered. Long deep sighs followed; of pain? of joy? Then silence. The yellow dress was still.

I fell back from the hedge in awe of what I had seen,

bewildered by what I had heard. What had happened? Was the girl now dead? But she had cried *Darling!* Not death then, but love had taken her. I remembered that woman and that man in the combe, those in the hop field, but I had heard no man's voice here, had seen nothing of his clothes beside the yellow dress. Was the man dumb and so inaudible? in a dark suit in the shadow of the hedge and so invisible? I turned again for signs of the man. None showed. And now, if the girl was not dead, she had surely fallen asleep.

I crept back to my clothes, put them on, then made my way along the hedge and the edges of the wheat to the field's gate. I climbed over and walked to the corner, to the further gate through which the girl must have gone, to which she would come. I leaned over, looked along the hedge but could see no one. I looked away to the hills, wondering on the girl, on the man in the dark suit.

The yellow of the girl's dress showed against the hedge. The girl came nearer until I could hear her again. *Her singing was like a swallow on a barn, and her mouth as sweet as a hoard of apples laid in hay.*[17]

With the help of Chaucer, I could tell of her singing, but only that silent man in the dark suit could tell of her mouth. I turned away until the girl was near, then turned again. No man walked by her side, nor behind her, nor was anyone in sight. Still singing, the girl walked with lazy grace to the gate. I opened it for her. She smiled, thanked me. I could now see that she was more than a girl, meaning that she was more than twenty. Her breasts strained against the yellow dress, bulged above it. She went through the gate with as much ease as her high heels allowed, went swaying beyond me, her bag swinging from her hand. She took up her song again. I watched her go. I shut the gate, climbed on it, sat staring at that point of the hedge from which she had come; where she had lain. *Whom* had she called 'Darling?' Was the man still there? I felt unease at the thought of him there, in a dark suit, silent in the shadows.

A screech tore the air, an animal cry. I spun around. The woman was running beside the hedge. She stopped. Then screamed.

I jumped down from the gate, ran to her side. Her hands were over her mouth, her eyes staring at a small rusty creature that hissed, spat, barked at her, weaving from side to side. 'My god!' she cried. 'O my god, what *is* it?'

'A stoat' I said, 'caught in a trap.' The iron teeth were clamped across its hindparts, imprisoning it while leaving its forepart free to sway from side to side in agony, to whip forward and back in anger: a dance of defiance. 'I'll have to kill it. I can't free it. It would die anyway. I'll *have* to kill it.' I turned and ran along the hedge for a heavy stick.

'Quick! Quick! *Kill* it. Oh, the poor thing' the woman cried. But when I raised the stick and struck, she cried 'No! No! *No!* Oh, don't, *don't.*' I hit the stoat again and again until it was still, its head smashed, its brains spilling out, its dance forever done. I hit it once again, uselessly, despairingly, then hurled the bloody stick away, then collapsed at the hedgeside, my head in my arms, trembling on the edge of tears, feeling sick.

The woman came to me, put her hand on my head, said, 'Don't go on. Don't go on so. You *had* to kill it. You said so. It couldn't have lived like that. You said so. You did a *good* deed, a kindness. Don't blame yourself. Don't go on so.'

She sat down beside me, put her arm about my shoulders. 'You did the only thing, dear. It was good of you, brave and kind of you.'

I looked up. The woman's eyes brimmed with tears, but she smiled, 'There now. That's better. You did *good.* It was awful to have to do it, but there's no pain now for the poor thing.'

I looked at the good I had done, at the body of the stoat, now still, beyond the pain of life.

Then, at the entrance to the old rabbit hole where the trap had been set, a small snout appeared, followed by a slim russet and white body. The woman saw it too. She leapt up with a cry. The stoat flashed back into the hole. 'The dead stoat's mate' I said.

'Oh my god' cried the woman jumping to her feet. 'I'm scared. I can't stand it. I . . . I've got to go . . .' She went stumbling over the field as fast as her heels allowed.

I sat looking on at the good I had done. The shining body with its bushy tail was still, but the head was already coming alive with flies. I could smell the death on which their lives depended.

The flies feasted. And not a few rabbits, if they could know of it, not a few rats and voles, would cheer and celebrate this death. No more would this stoat dance attendance on their ends, rolling on the ground before them, darting, hopping, hurling himself into the air as if to entertain them before drawing near and nearer, until the final leap, his teeth at their throats, their last screams.

The stoat was a killer, but I could find no comfort in having put an end to his dance, could gain no peace from the good I had done. *I* was now a killer.

One God made the rabbit and the stoat that tore at the rabbit's throat; the same God made men who set murderous traps; the same God made a boy with a horror of such traps . . . only to make a murderer of *him.* And it was that boy's death-dealing that now made it possible for innumerable flies to feed, fatten, live — to what end? To feed and fatten the spider in the hedge, waiting in the corner of his web.

I had no such thought at the time, only the dullest ache. I sat a little way from the stink and buzz about the dead stoat, bewilderingly aware that I was also caught in a web whose strands ran in all directions, in opposite ways often and to no certain end: good deeds could lead to bad ends; bad deeds to good. I had done 'good' but felt bad about it. I could not explain it any more than I could understand how that woman had cried *Darling!* yet had been alone all the while; how she had cried out in apparent pain, had moaned, had groaned, yet come away smiling, swaying, singing.

I remembered her arm about my shoulders. The woman had called me *Dear*. Lying on her back on the other side of the hedge, whom had she called *Darling!*

Already in my short life I had had acquaintance with the ambiguous ways of God: His brambles gave sweet berries and drew blood; His black bryony showed flowers as yellow as a girl's summer dress, and heart-shaped leaves that would wither in time to leave red berries for a child to pick, be poisoned by them, be paralysed. God in His high heaven made the sun and the moon, brought all things to life, only to have them die; made humankind and then demanded human sacrifice, as He had done of his own Son. God made small guileless creatures and cunning ones to kill them, and yet more cunning men to kill these. Then made a boy with the wish to be kind to all creatures, who then, out of that very wish, must himself kill.

Clearly the ways of God surpassed all possible understanding. God wore a *very* dark suit. One might well kneel in awe; in fear and trembling bow one's head. But one could *not* lie back on the earth and cry out to high heaven, *'Darling! Darling! Darling!'*

With the end of that summer, I went back to school to learn more Latin verbs, more of the cunning of princes and the properties of gases. I learned nothing that in any way answered my wonder over that woman alone and yet in the throes of love; nothing to justify the ways of the God who had reigned over that summer afternoon. Every Sunday the Priest gave assurance that God was only and always good. Recalling the scream of the stoat, the smell of its death, I wondered.

Another summer came and went; another spring with the sap rising in me so that I longed for release, for some kind of realization, some flowering, some fruit. Cold baths on rising could not calm, nor running nor rugby exhaust, nor scripture lessons contain my longing.

Another school year ended. Another summer came. I wandered far and wide over the moor, flung myself down often and often as if to ease that ache — for what I did not know, for which I could find no words.

On Alice's shelves, I found a book called *Far Away and Long Ago*. I read: *And that was the life I desired – the life the heart can conceive: the earth life.*[18] Was that what I desired? Earth life? But what was that? And how could I come upon it? Not far away and long ago, but here and now, in Somerset, this summertime.

Man had fallen through woman's fault, the Bible said. Both woman and man were now barred from Paradise. So be it. I had no wish to return to an old Garden ruled over by God, the Great *Thou-Shalt-Not!* Nor did I wish for any future in another world, but only to be *here,* wholly, for here and now, I sensed, was a world of ease and shining if only *I* was here, if only I could *see* it — a world without a stern God, with shy deer and a Serpent and Eve in the guise of a girl in search of a youth such as I was; so that with the half she was and the half I was, we might make a whole, might each thereby *be* whole — a state of being that would make Eden of any ordinary garden, of any common place. *There is another world but it is in this one.*[19] I could not see it, but I sensed it: the sky was innocent, with no more evil than a lone buzzard in pursuit of life; the moor was open, green, innocent with wild ponies, with shy deer; the Serpent was surely there: I had seen adders in May, mating. Only Eve was missing.

A green hill I once lay on, in memory became a girl I lay on — the first: a freckled girl with the up-turned nose of a child and a long golden plait. One day I dared to pull her down by that plait and lay beside her in wonder of our being together at that moment in that place, haunted by invisible Eden.

Long ago I had learned a little of what lay darkly under the bright daisies of the girl's skirt, but I had been to school since then. The girl had also been to school. 'How hot it is', she sighed and undid the top button of her blouse. It was hotter than that but she did not undo any more buttons, and I did not dare. I had been to schools for boys only, so that, except in dreams, I was dolefully shy.

I turned on my side and pulled from a back pocket the creased pages of *The Song of Songs,* torn from a Bible and so freed from all the bloodshed, greed, fear and grim prophecies that went before and came after. I read aloud: *Let him kiss me with the kisses of his mouth; for thy love is better than wine. Thine ointments have goodly fragrance. Thy name is as an ointment poured forth; therefore do the virgins love thee.*

The girl deeply sighed, shifted in the warm grass, softened. I read on, winning her by another's words. But while I sensed her waiting and her willingness, I did not dare her red mouth. I turned on my belly, put my hands only upon the hill, took hold of the grass. The girl lay at my side, silent, staring at the sky.

It happened so, or similarly, the next afternoon: the same hill, another poet. Again the girl lay on her back. Again I lay on my belly on the earth beside her, even though I knew that the next day would be our last, and the girl would go as far away as Manchester and soon be long ago.

Before the bedroom mirror that night I cursed my cowardice, then turned away, turned off the light, went naked to bed to dream of all I would do in the light of the next day. I vowed it, turned on my side and slept. Full of the same fierce resolve, I rose next morning a Don Juan out of my dreams, so that when the girl that afternoon lay back upon the hill, made a pillow of her hands, pointed her elbows to the sky, lifting her small breasts like quinces under the sun, I dared at last to do a little of what I had dreamed to do: I kissed her with the kisses of my mouth; with wild arms about her, trembled on her until tea-time.

The next morning she was gone.

I was in London for a few days before the next school term began. In the midst of much activity, I would sometimes be still and wonder upon the coming of love —

in which grey terraced house lived that glowing girl? out of which window would my Lady lean? up which drainpipe should I climb to be beside her in the blessed dark . . . until the milkman called.

In the crowded streets, I walked by my wild lone, longed for the empty moor and, in that summer city, sang with the anonymous poet:

O western wind, when wilt thou blow,
that the small rain down can rain?
Christ! that my love were in my arms
and I in my bed again.

I who had never had a girl in bed.

For lack of a girl in bed, I found one in a book: the wild girl, Rima, of Hudson's *Green Mansions*.

A man in that book wandered into a dark tropical forest. I recognized the country of my own mind — the hanging vines, undergrowth and tanglewood, the heat, the black shadows. I forgot the green hill, the freckled girl with the golden plait, and dreamed myself into a far-away forest, with the hope of hearing among the high trees the whistle and call of the bird-girl, Rima. As the book told: *I soon became entangled in a dense undergrowth, which so confused me that at last I confessed despairingly to myself that for the first time in this wood I was hopelessly lost.* The hero of the book asked, *'Where was I?'* I asked the same.

One day I walked into Hyde Park in the spirit of pilgrimage to see the memorial to the creator of Rima. I stood long and still and gazed at Rima rising with the great birds on either side of her.

A young woman came and stood by my side. With the help of my imagination she could be made dark enough; her skirt and blouse could be changed, even removed. She was some years older and a little taller than I, but imagination soon made a 'Man' of me, and of her: Rima herself, returned to the world; a phoenix out of the forest fire that had consumed her far away and long ago, to be at my side now in a London park.

I was still. I said nothing, felt no need to say anything. When the young woman turned to go, I imagined that she smiled at me a little; it was enough for me to *know* that she had. She went. I looked after her, saw how the dark river of hair poured down her savage back. I did not pursue her. I expected her going. As the good book said: *to keep her near me always in sight was, I found, impossible: she would be free as the wind, free as the butterfly, going and coming at her wayward will, and losing herself from sight a dozen times every hour.*

I turned back to the memorial, and smiled. It had happened. I was sure of it, and was as sure of her return next day. At the same time the next day I waited before the stone girl, repeating from the book: *Rima, you are like all beautiful things in the wood – flower and bird, and butterfly, and green leaf, and frond, and little silky-haired monkey high up in the trees . . . And when I listen to Rima's voice, talking in a language I cannot understand, I hear the wind whispering in the leaves.*

A whispering in the leaves was all that I heard. The young woman never came. A big woman came; much older, with a small thin man. The woman guffawed at Rima. The man giggled, pointed to her naked breasts and below. I had read how other men had daubed this memorial to The Man Who Loved Birds with tar, feathers and swastikas.

The couple left. I gripped the rail and asked aloud of Rima, 'Where am I? Where can I be? In such a world, where *can* I be?'

The next day made it clear: I was back at school. *In that wood there is one law that Rima imposes, and outside of it is a different law.*

I obeyed this different law as best I could. I read the required books, took Shakespeare and Milton apart, while I took whole, by torchlight under the blankets at night, tales of far-away places, wondering all the while where in the world I would find myself. It seemed certain that the answer to my whereabouts lay far away from the confines of an English public school. In all spare and stolen moments

I dreamed of islands, sailed a small boat over great seas to beach where a brown girl stood waiting on my coming, saying as Rima: *I am here; now you know where you are.*

Winter came and spring. Set against the lively season was the dead weight of all I had to read, to swallow, to hold and to spew out later in an examination room.

News of the result came in the summer holiday. My vomit had been rewarded: I had passed the examination with honours. I ran over the moor to Dunkery Beacon and looked more than a hundred miles in every direction: Dartmoor to the south, east to the Quantock Hills, west to the Burrows, north to Horner Wood and beyond, over the water to Wild Wales, the Black Mountains. The world was before me. I was free. I lay on my back under the circling of a pair of buzzards; their high excited cries echoed in me.

As the sun dropped I started home. It was then that I realized I was *not* free. This one examination only made way for further examinations: in two years I would take another to gain entrance to a University where I would be submitted to more exams, more swallowing, holding, spewing out, more vomiting.

I walked blind and deaf to all about me until I heard a curlew cry of another world in this one: a wild cry, a call I must obey. I could not go on, would *not* go on and on in the way of these past years.

I was silent over supper. Alice glanced at me often but said nothing until, at the end, 'What's the matter, Michael? You went so happily out of the house this morning.'

I bit my lip. 'I can't go on, Alice. I *can't*. I can't go on with school.'

'What is it you want to do?'

I was a long while silent, then said, 'I don't know, Alice. I don't know. I want to *live*. I don't know what that means but I want to *live*.' How would I explain the cry of that curlew? I would tell only of a want to wander the world, to go free and further than the confines of a University's walls, to walk by my wild lone . . . I could only say to Alice,

'But it's not just wandering I want. I don't know *what* I want. I *know* I don't want to go back to school.'

'Then you shall not.'

'You mean I don't *have* to go back to school?'

'You don't have to go back to school,' said Alice. 'You know that I have never been happy about your schooling, but I've followed your father's plans. Now with your exam over, we can change course. Little good can come of forcing you to go on and on in the same way.'

I went with Alice to see my Headmaster. He was grave, cold, polite: 'If you'll excuse my saying so, this seems to me a very foolish decision.'

Alice smiled, 'Of course, it is. I *am* a fool. The point is: what about Michael? Is he or isn't he a fool? If he is not, then he should go on here. If he *is* a fool, then he should go his own way, persisting in his folly.'

I remembered a quote that had been pinned to a cupboard: *If the fool would persist in his folly, he would become wise.* But the Headmaster had forgotten or did not approve of William Blake. He saw a mad woman before him and threw up his hands. I walked out of the brown study with Alice, out of the school gates for the last time.

I was not done with schooling, however; only with that school. Alice had often spoken of another at Dartington in Devon. She had always wished me to go there, and I had walked in its grounds with her in spring under the great trees rising out of rings of crocuses and daffodils; in the bright of summer, the brown and gold of autumn, in winter grey.

'You say you don't know what to do' Alice pointed out, 'so that it seems a little early for you to go out into the world. We've agreed that you don't have to go back to school. But Dartington is not what you mean by *school*.' She held out a pamphlet. Read this and see if you want to know more about Dartington.'

I lay on the lawn and read: *This school is for adventure. It is commonly believed that except for the South Pole, the Himalayas, and the scientific laboratory, fields of adventure are closed. In earlier days man set out to discover new lands, to build empires, to fight battles, to promote business enterprise, or to develop industry. The driving force behind such adventure was almost inevitably some single dominating personality, king, general or merchant adventurer. Today adventure assumes, perforce, a more social character; it must be undertaken in cooperation with others and not at their expence. Such possibilities of adventure are assuredly inherent in everyday life, and nowhere does such a promising field exist as that in the hearts of children who, with their fresh powers of intelligence, invention, imagination and enterprise, embrace in themselves all the elements necessary for adventurous living. It is our aim to provide an environment in which children can exercise these powers, both as individuals and as members of a group, so that education and adventure can be hardly distinguishable.*[20]

I took the pamphlet back to Alice. 'I'd like to know more about Dartington.' Alice told me many things, even that I did not have to take any exams there, nor even attend classes. She was joking, of course. 'But no' said Alice. 'You don't have to take my word for it. You can ask Bill Curry, the Headmaster. You'll find he's not what you mean by a *Headmaster*. We can go and see him, see the school, so that you can make up your own mind.'

Instead of a 'Headmaster,' I found at Dartington a small round leprechaun of a man with a large bald head; smiling and fond, unlike any master, any man I had known. He seemed half the size of Alice, but in no way wanting in presence. Indeed, after she had spoken a while, Bill Curry, with a smile, put Alice in her place: 'Alice, I know that *you've* always wanted Michael to come here. But what does Michael want?'

'I want to come here, if you'll have me, Sir.' I said that I had read the prospectus. Alice added, 'You had a question to ask, Michael.'

I hesitated, then said, 'I understand that one doesn't even have to attend classes here.'

'That's true' said Bill Curry. 'You'll find only a few things that you *have* to do, and those are things that you, with all others here, pupils and staff, have agreed to do for the good of all.' He explained that all rules were made by fortnightly meetings of The Moot, a kind of parliament where everyone — smallest boy or girl or Headmaster — had equal vote. Rules, necessary for any community, were made by one and all and only for as long as they worked. If found not to work, they were scrapped, and new ones agreed upon for trial.

I had read: *This school is for adventure*. Even, I happily thought, for *anarchy*.

That autumn, at my own wish, I went alone by train to Totnes. A man in the carriage, hearing that I was going to Dartington Hall, said, 'Oh, that's the place where boys and girls all swim together, isn't it? in their birthday suits!'

Was it possible? *This school is for adventure* . . . for not attending classes or taking exams; it was for swimming together, girls and boys, naked as Eve and as Adam. It sounded like Paradise.

Bill Curry picked me up at the station. I shook his hand, said , 'How do you do, Sir?' Bill Curry smiled, 'I'm no *Sir*. Just Bill.' He drove me out of town, turned over a small humped bridge into a place of open fields and tall trees, then turned off the road to Foxhole, the senior school. A girl sat in Curry's room, reading a book. Curry introduced us, then said to the girl, 'I'll see you shortly, Jessica, but would you first take Michael to his room? And let him meet Pia?'

I went with Jessica into an inner courtyard to find boys and girls in a wide, sometimes wild, variety of clothing. One boy was wearing a tophat. 'What's he wearing that for?'

'Because he wants to' said Jessica.

'You mean you can wear anything you like here?'

'Why not?'

I imagined myself in a tophat, just a tophat, a tophat and my 'birthday suit.' No wonder Alice liked this place. Everyone was a bit mad. I belonged here.

Jessica showed me to my room. *My* room! After years of crowded dormitories, I stared around. A room of one's own! Then out of the window, I saw a dark girl across the courtyard climb out of a window and take the hand of the fair boy who had called her. 'Is one allowed to do that?'

'Do what?'

'Climb out of the window and . . .'

'It's the quickest way into the courtyard' Jessica pointed out.

I wanted to ask more: that boy hand-in-hand with the girl, for instance . . . Would Jessica say only that it was the loveliest way? the most loving?

'Let's go and see Pia' said Jessica.

'*Pia*? What a strange name. Who's she?'

'She's your Housemother. She's half Italian, half Irish. Her other name's Malone. She's . . .' Jessica hesitated, smiled a little mysteriously, added, 'Well, you'll see.'

Pia Malone's room was a little way down the corridor. Her door was open, but she was not in. 'She's out walking, I expect. Or painting' said Jessica. She left.

I went back to my room, lay on the bed and marvelled at my being there. It was like no school I had known, like none I could ever have imagined. *A school for adventure* seemed a contradiction; it was at any rate a paradox. Trust Alice!

I sat on the bed, looked out onto the sunlit courtyard, then got up and leaned out of the window into the light. It was like peering into the centre of those paintings by Alice. If it was not a Garden, it was not walled about either, nor in any way denied me by teachers, preachers, rules and regulations, angry angels, flaming swords. I was free at any moment to climb out of the window into that sunlit world, to walk there by my wild lone; or with another, hand-in-hand, as dark as I was fair; a girl as dark as Jessica, as Israel, as an Indian *ayah,* as a gypsy somewhere in a secret valley, sloe-eyed, gentle, wild.

6 PIA

I am the angel of reality,
Seen for a moment standing in the door.
. . . I am the necessary angel of earth
Since, in my sight, you see the earth again.
Wallace Stevens

WHENEVER, IN THE YEARS AFTER, I WISHED TO tell of Pia Malone, the wish gave rise to the image of her; that image made me silent. The known facts of her life were, moreover, few and they seemed unremarkable. Happiness does not make history, nor even a reasonable story, being out of reason's reach.

As a painter can show light only by showing the things it lights upon, so I can tell of Pia Malone only by telling of myself — here is history, for here is folly. Light falls on fools as on the wise; the difference between these is a difference of shadows; the light is one and is otherwise.

Some facts of my time at Dartington may therefore serve to celebrate Pia Malone. They might do more, for I have since come to see that the light was not hers. If I am at all able to tell of Pia, I will have told of transparency: how, when we no longer stand in the way, the Light in us lightens all things.

Attempts to tell the untellable have given rise to fairy tales, myths and legends. Rooted in fact and in history, their enduring power lies in the possibility of their happening even now, even to each of us. The tale of *Beauty and the Beast* will have been told us in our childhood; later it may be reported in a local paper; it can happen in our town, in our time, in us — surely, it *must* sometime happen in us if we are ever to be whole; allowing the beast we are, even as the beauty: animal and angel, both.

Were Aphrodite and Hecate only in the imagination of the Greeks of long ago? Who then this midnight calls, 'Hullo, darling' from a shadowed doorway in Soho? We may have haunting sight of Helen at a country fair, or fleeting, unforgettable glimpse of Beatrice in a busy street. It happened in this way for an Italian poet one May morning on a bridge in Florence in the year 1283.

In its own way and measure, more than six centuries after, it happened so for an English schoolboy one September afternoon in Dartington, Devon — the sudden alarming sight of Woman, of *the Eternal Feminine that leads us on;*[21] even some inkling of that to which we are led: that Silence we shatter by the name 'God,' that Space we fill.

A grown man, I came to realize this. At the time I was but a boy of sixteen, bewildered by sudden inexplicable light in the world.

I climbed out of the window of my room at Dartington, turned to the walnut tree in the corner of the courtyard, put my hand on it a moment, then went into the building beyond. An open door showed paintings on the walls, and shelves of clay and wooden sculptures in various stages of completion. I walked into the room a few paces, then stopped.

The sun streamed into the room through tall windows. In the farthest corner sat a woman in a blue skirt and peasant blouse that showed white against her sunbrowned neck, the slope of her shoulders, her arms. Her hair was long and fair, pulled loosely back from her face. Her head in profile was that of an old coin, brightly burnished; with the sun full upon her she seemed *made* of light. She sat on a high stool, her hands together in her lap, looking to the hills. If she had heard me, she gave no sign of it; made no move, no sound. There was no sound in the room, in all the world.

I had stopped at first sight of her, my breath held. A constriction in my chest moved up to my throat, as though a hand was around it. I could not have spoken even if I had wished. I had no wish. I could only stand there.

I say that *I* stood there. At the time there was no one, only silence, only stillness in the room and in all it showed of the woman, of my own body and being, of walls and sunlit windows, stools, tables, chairs, easels and all else, even as the surrounding hills and fields, the unclouded sky, the sun — all seen at once and whole, as one of the paintings on the wall, but with an added dimension, with a hardly bearable reality.

It was so, I later supposed, for half a minute. I could as meaningfully speak of a full minute, an hour, a day, a year, a lifetime even, even of eternity. I could speak of a moment out of time, or something such, and make it sound miraculous or mystical. But I wish to speak of facts only: of the woman, simply, with the sun on her, sitting in that room on a stool, still, looking out onto fields and far-away hills, her hands in her lap.

The woman turned and looked at me. Had she all the while known that I was there? She faced me now without surprise, without greeting or acknowledgement. She simply looked. After a moment she smiled — a little. She said nothing.

I said nothing. My eyes pained with repressed tears. I could say nothing, do nothing. Suddenly I felt I would fall and to save myself took small hesitant steps backwards to the door, my hand on a table for support. I could not take my eyes off the woman until I was out of the door, freed from her steady gaze. Even then I walked some paces backward before I turned and went, as though drugged or dreaming, down the long corridor.

My room was as I had left it, but now had something of the silence, space and light of that other room. The curtains were more yellow than they had been; the woodgrain on the cupboard *flowed;* the whole room had in some extraordinary way come *alive.* I had also come alive — not 'I,' but the seeing, the hearing, in all ways sensing. In awe and some alarm I stood at the door, then made for the bed and lay down. I found reassurance in its firmness, in the roughness of the woven bedspread under my hand.

What had happened? What was happening? What . . .? I began to wonder, to think. The quickened senses dulled, leaked away. The light went from the room. The curtains were bright yellow again, but only bright yellow, no longer irradiant. The grain of the cupboard showed a fixed flat pattern. In the language of the old myth and in the imagery of Alice: the Garden faded from sight; the Gate closed. I was outside the Wall again.

And not sorry to be so. The haunting sense of loss was balanced by a reassuring return of my old 'self,' and of the familiar world. A boy ran down the corridor shouting, 'Tea-time! time for tea!' I got off the bed, went to the small mirror in fear of seeing a stranger, in hope of finding someone I had known all my life. Relieved, I opened the door, walked to the dining-room wondering what would surprise more: to see that Woman again, sipping tea, and so to know that I had for a moment inhabited another world, or *not* to see her and so to understand that I had only dreamed: that there was no such Woman, no such world.

I got a tray of food. Jessica hailed me from a table. I went to her. She introduced me to David, who had his arm about the back of her chair, and to others there, including Jan Sangorsky, the boy I had seen in a tophat. He now sported a beret.

'Finding your way around?' asked David. I nodded.

'I'd forgotten it was Pia's day off' said Jessica. 'So we shouldn't disturb her. I'll take you to see her tomorrow. Or you can go to her room and introduce yourself.' She pointed to another table. 'That's her.' The Woman was sipping tea, eating bread and butter.

'I'll go to her room tomorrow' I said. I added: 'You said *Pia is* . . . But then you stopped and said only: *You'll see* . . . What did you mean?'

Jan said 'You'll see the Snow Queen in her cave of ice.'

Jessica laughed, 'Don't worry about Jan. He's in love with Pia.'

'In love with Pia! Am I bloody hell! I want a woman of flesh and blood, a wild woman, hot, passionate . . .'

'You'd run a mile from such a woman' said David.

Jan opened his mouth in protest, then shut it in a wry smile. 'You may be right, but that's the kind of woman I'd *like* to run from — not too fast, so that she'd catch me. But I can run after Pia any time. Any one can. Everyone here *does.* But if anyone ever caught her, he'd embrace a cloud. Pia's a *myth.*'

David asked, 'Why then does she disturb you so?'

'She *doesn't* disturb me. Facts disturb, flesh and blood disturb, not phantoms. It's just that she's . . . she's . . . Oh hell!' Jan turned to me. 'As Jessica said, you'll see. You'll find out.'

I went the next morning to see Pia, but saw from the open door that her room was full of girls and boys. I went later to find fewer people but enough to discourage me. The next time I tried, the door was shut. I knocked. At Pia's call, I went in.

Pia sat on the floor with a girl; a spread of postcard reproductions of paintings before them. Pia smiled up at me, 'We've already met.' She introduced me to the girl, then asked her to leave us a while; to leave the postcards if she would. I sat on the floor in the girl's place. Pia explained that the girl had brought them back from a holiday in Paris. She remarked how good the colours were, then asked which paintings among them moved me. I pointed to one by Bonnard of a woman in a bath.

'Because it's a wonderful painting? or because you like women in baths?'

'Both' I said shyly. 'I also like his others — ordinary things, a view from a window, a table, a tree.' I told Pia that I had seen a number of reproductions of paintings by Bonnard in books belonging to my Aunt Alice. I pointed to other cards: an early Picasso, a Modigliani, a Gauguin that I had not seen before — mostly of women, naked or nearly so — but then, Rouault's *Clown*. 'One of my favourite painters isn't here, and probably wouldn't be in Paris: Samuel Palmer.'

'Samuel Palmer!' Pia showed some surprise, but then went on to speak of some of the other cards there, by painters unknown to me.

I was not listening. I was looking at Pia. As she bent over the cards I could see, beyond the low curve of her blouse, her brown-gold breasts. *Such beauty, dear God! O God, such beauty!* I said it over and over within me, not noticing that Pia had stopped talking. Unknown to me she had lifted her head. After a moment, she asked, 'Michael, are you undressing me?' I did not answer. I closed my eyes, bit my lip.

'Michael,' called Pia quietly. She reached out and put her hand on my tight fist. I looked up. She was smiling, 'It's all right, Michael. I don't mind. Why shouldn't you?' She sat still some while. To let me look on? I looked down.

Pia got to her feet. 'Come' she said. 'The sun's already warm. Have you swum yet? Shall we? I'm sure some of the others will come.'

I got up and went to my room. I remembered that man in the train saying, 'Dartington Hall? That's where the boys and girls swim together, isn't it? in their birthday suits!' I took up a towel and, uncertainly, my costume.

Pia's call: 'Anyone for a swim?' opened doors. The cry went up, 'Swimming! Swimming!' We gathered in Pia's room, then went together out of the house. The others leapt and rushed down the flight of steps towards the field where the pool lay.

A girl broke away, began to run. A boy gave chase. Still running, the girl pulled her blouse over her head, dropped it on the grass, ran on, naked from the waist up. The boy pulled off his shirt, flung it from him. Soon everyone was following their lead, running and stripping as they ran — blouses, shirts, skirts and trousers, underwear of all kinds and colours were scattered on the grass. They called, shouted, ran naked at the end, laughed and leapt onto the low mound that separated the field from the pool, then hurled themselves into the water.

I did not run after them. Smiling, I walked at Pia's side to the edge of the pool, whispering, It's Eden. It's Eden! I turned to say it aloud to Pia, but was made silent by her bared breasts. She was undoing her skirt. I unbuttoned my shirt, watching Pia pull the last covering from her hips. She went to the pool, dived in . I hurried to undress, smiled at my costume on the grass, plunged in.

After the swim, the others stood in the sun drying themselves, twisting, turning, laughing, shaking the water from their heads, their bodies glowing from the rough towels. One by one they went across the green fields back to the house, bending as they came upon their scattered clothes until, fully dressed again, they climbed the stone steps.

Pia and I dressed by the pool, then walked slowly back. Nothing was said until we reached the door of Pia's room. There, I said 'Thank you, Miss Malone.'

'Pia' she said.

'Thank you, Pia.'

She smiled conspiratorially.

I did not have to attend classes. For two days I did not. The others did. They waved to me as I went by their classrooms, then turned back to whatever they were doing. It seemed that I was missing something. On the third day I went into lessons and, with the knowledge that I could leave at any time, I stayed. There was reason to stay: learning here was not imposed from above: it was an experience in which all shared, teacher as pupils. Exceptions to this were also recognized. Jan was eager to study, but not with others. He worked under direction, alone in the library or in his room. To each according to his kind, according to his needs.

Alice had said that Dartington was not what was

ordinarily meant by a 'school.' I wondered how a master at my last school would have responded to a boy and a girl listening to him with their arms about one another as, through a classroom window, I saw Jessica and David?

Alice had said that Bill Curry was not what one ordinarily meant by a 'Headmaster.' The school in his charge and care was only one aspect of a larger undertaking that included forestry, a weaving mill, a farm, a cider press, crafts of all kinds, a dance and music school, a theatre, and much else. Some of the commercial departments expressed concern over the effect that rumours to which the school gave rise might have on their own successful outcome. The school's image was often reduced in the public eye to the fact that boys and girls swam together in the 'altogether,' lived and slept in the same house; in the minds of not a few, slept in the same bed.

To answer such concern, Bill Curry called an evening meeting. It was not attended by pupils, so that it was some years later that I read of it. One of the questions asked: *Does the school encourage, condone, or ignore sexual intercourse among the children?*

A part of Bill Curry's denial told that: *Dartington takes love affairs among children for granted. The word 'silly' is never used in order to discourage flirting. Love in adolescence is normal, and ought therefore to be welcomed as a sign of normal development.*[22] He was later to say: *To have one's sexual manifestations dealt with in childhood and in youth so that some degree of permanent aversion or shame is generated is wholly wrong. And yet how often must this have been done. One must succeed in making clear why the impulses must be controlled in the present, without suggesting in the very least that they are intrinsically regrettable. Control should be suggested now in a way which does nothing to prejudice future delight.*[23]

Fine words that might have met the usual fate of fine words. How they survived at Dartington was made clear by Jessica's story.

Jessica had from the start showed a sisterly interest in

the shy boy that I was; her David also befriended me. Sitting with them one day, I spoke of the wonder of finding myself in a school where Jessica and David could go hand in hand, even embrace in the bright sun of the courtyard. I wondered where the school 'drew the line.'

'It doesn't draw hard and fast lines' said David.

'You mean that you can *really* do what you want?'

'If you *really* want to' said Jessica with a smile. 'I'll tell you a story.' She turned to David, 'May I? If Michael keeps it to himself?' David nodded.

Jessica told how one night she left her room for David's room and his bed. They lay in one another's arms. There was a knock on the door. Jessica slipped down the bed, pulled the covers over her head. David called 'Come in.' Pia came in, saw the lump that was Jessica, smiled, sat on the end of the bed. She patted the lump, 'Come up for air, Jessica.' Jessica emerged and at once started to get out of the bed. Pia reached forward, pressed Jessica back. She spoke to Jessica and David then of their love for one another, and so of the naturalness of their being together in bed as now, of wanting one another, of wanting to make love.

'David and I had never made love' said Jessica. 'I told Pia so.' Pia answered that it would be enough for it to become known that they were in bed together; that if only in view of David's liveliness and of Jessica's loveliness, few would believe that they had been in bed and *not* made love — and, she added, they would not call it 'love.' Outside the school was a world of men and women, many of whom had grown old without love and so were envious of young people in love. Such men and women would pounce on a possibility of the 'immorality' they sought and so relished. They would have the school closed, finding compensation and justification for their own lovelessness in morality, virtue, righteousness.

'She didn't make us feel in any way bad' said David. 'On the contrary. But she *did* make us realize that our care for each other must include everybody: the school, too.'

'And that was *all*' added Jessica. 'She didn't tell me to get out of David's bed and go back to my room. All she said was, "I'm for bed." She touched my cheek: 'Goodnight, Jessica.' She touched David's hand: 'Goodnight, David.' She got off the bed and went out of the room, leaving us there.'

'She let you stay in bed together?'

'She let us stay in bed together' said Jessica. 'But I didn't stay. Nor did David want me to. I kissed David. There was no hurry. We didn't feel furtive or guilty any more. David held me. Then he let me go. I went back to my room. I haven't been in David's bed since.' She reached for David's hand, smiled and said 'We can wait.' She added, 'Pia never mentioned the incident again. She seemed to forget all about it. David and I never have, never will.'

Jessica's story, as all others I heard about Pia, fuelled my interest. The search for meaning that accompanies adolescence, the need to know what life was about, and how to go about it, became in large part my need to understand Pia. Clearly she *knew*. It was not so much her words that made this clear; her words were few. It was as much and more, the way she walked or was still, the way she looked at things, at others, at me. The way she smiled, slightly, as with some secret knowledge held from me, not for lack of knowing but for want of being.

What was it she knew? What moved her? What was Pia's secret? the source of her serenity? of her gentle strength? In what Ground was she so deeply rooted that she could live so lightly, so *invisibly,* yet here and now, vulnerable as a willow in all winds? To what sky, to what source of light did she owe her transparency? What flowered in her as calm? as care-less care for others, for all things — weeping children, wounded creatures, even broken teacups, even old brooms?

I asked such questions of those who had known Pia longer. I only learned more of the meaning of paradox. Pia was 'sort of religious' said one girl. 'But she has no religion' a boy pointed out. Pia never mentioned God, did not believe in Him, it seemed, but this was not to say that she disbelieved. She neither believed or disbelieved, having *faith,* we decided. But faith in what? No one could say. Perhaps it was not a matter of faith, but of fact? *What* fact? What did she *know,* and so wholly know it that she *was* it?

Pia expressed no fixed views, no values. She responded to each situation as it arose. *Should* and *ought* were not words she used. She responded but did not react. She did not judge. She expressed preferences sometimes, but no likes, no dislikes. This did not make her lukewarm. Joy showed in her readily as sorrow, but somehow it was not *her* joy, *her* sorrow; it was simply that joy or sorrow was the nature of things at the moment, and she responded with smiling or with tears. But only for the moment. Nothing lived on in her beyond its time. She had no moods.

As far as anyone knew, Pia had had an unremarkable past. The facts of her life could in no way account for her being. She showed no interest in the future, had no ambitions or wishes that could seem to give shape or direction to her days. She was at all times present.

Even that must be qualified by the question: *Who* was present? Can an Absence be present? can it be *Presence?* Is space present? Absent herself, Pia made space for all others, for all things; she was space for them to grow in, to be in.

Some of us would gather in Pia's room at the day's end to set the world aright; sometimes taking sides in heated argument. Pia would sit among us, sewing or drawing, or just sitting, saying nothing; smiling sometimes with that little smile of hers. I would at times be even more than ordinarily aware of her; and at once fall silent. Sometimes we would all become aware of her; the argument would slow, falter, lapse. Sometimes we would turn to her for her comment. What she said could seem to favour both sides, or neither; so that they cancelled out, leaving silence.

Sometimes she would not answer at all, only smile, and in the light of that, our solemn dispute no longer seemed to matter. Or she would say a few words, or only one, or make some small gesture that seemed so full of meaning that we would wait on her for fuller explanation. None would be given. There would be that half-smile again, so that we would wonder if she had meant what she had said, had even said it at all — her words, her gestures, seemed to come from no one, arise out of nothing, out of nowhere . . . and return there.

What did Pia *mean,* not only by her words at any one time, but by her *being* always? My adolescence, made solemn by the search for meaning, allowed little simply to *be.*

For Pia it seemed, the being of things was all. She seemed to have no need of meaning: facts were enough: the simple fact of what was before her at each moment; not the 'good' or the 'bad' of things, but only the hard fact or the soft of them, the long or short; the fact of rock, of water, of sky, of the way things *are,* here and now. I later read the philosopher Wittgenstein, saying: *It is not* how *things are in the world that is mystical, but* that *it exists.* But Pia was no philosopher. She was a *presence.*

That presence was not always pleasing. A girl came storming out of Pia's room one day crying 'She's a bitch, a heartless *bitch.* She doesn't care about anyone.' The girl lived dramatically always; in depths of gloom or heights of ecstasy. Pia would not have indulged her. In time the girl's passion gave way to a cold determination to 'tell Pia a few truths about herself.' She returned to Pia's room, only to emerge later with tears running down her cheeks, saying 'She's a saint, an *angel!* Oh, why can't *I* be like her? Why? Why? *Why?*'

The girl's disturbance passed. Jan Sangorsky's lasted. Jan had come to Dartington only a few months before me, after a succession of schools had rejected him. His father, a brilliant intellectual who taught philosophy at a university was, by Jan's account, emotionally immature. Jan's mother had left his father. Jan could understand this, but could not forgive her abandonment of him; nor could Jan find compensation in his father's consequent habit of wives and mistresses. Jan had suffered a surfeit of 'mothers.' His background made him a rebel against all male rule and bitter about women. 'Love,' he informed me with grave authority, 'is glandular, a simple matter of chemical secretions.' With a grin, he added, 'Trouble is, we all have glands.' Jan's saving grace was his sense of humour, though it was often black and twisted, often turned against himself.

Dartington did little to allow the aggressive stance that was Jan's armour. Bill Curry offered little authority to oppose. Jan could freely swear or wear his several hats, with little notice taken. His conviction about the wiles and ways of all women was undermined by the women about him. It did not save him from one small, frail, gentle girl who moved him, he confessed to me, 'to the very bowels' — his great hands reached into the air as though to cup and cover her virginal breasts. My good friend Jan was a foul-mouthed atheistical Jew with the enormous hands of a strangler; suffering his gentle heart and using strong words to hide it. His hand clasp was weak and hesitant as though, in offering his hand, he feared one might take it. He needed that hand for his one passion, painting.

That passion brought him daily into the presence of Pia. He complained, 'I wish to God we had a *man* to teach art.'

'Why?'

'That woman is distracting. She's so damn . . . Oh, I don't know what, but she's *damnable.* She's not beautiful' he pointed out. 'She *isn't.* Her nose is too long, her brow too high, too wide. Her eyes . . .'

'She disturbs you.'

'Me?' he protested. Then grinned, 'Yes, she does. That's what I mean: she's a distraction. She's so bloody immaculate, so . . . so *virginal.*' It came from him as a term of abuse, but then shaking his head, he added, 'That's not true either. She *must* know all about it, and at first hand, because she's unshockable. I've tried to shock her.' He told how, standing at Pia's side, he had shown her a drawing by George Grosz of a lecherous pig-headed man with a fat whore at his side. He told Pia that he wholly identified with the man; told what he would like to do to the whore. 'I wanted to shock her, but she turned and looked at me, just *looked;* the way she does. Then she smiled in some secret knowing way . . . I swear it was a *whore's* way!'

Another day, Jan burst into my room to complain of Pia's comments on his work. 'She was right,' he admitted, 'but I wouldn't admit it to her. What annoys me is that while she only talks about the painting, I get the feeling that she's talking about *me,* as though my painting was not simply what I do, but what I *am.* I like painting. I don't like what I am, and I don't want to be reminded of it. They're different things. God damn her!' His face darkened, '*Fuck* her!'

I was shocked. I had heard the word often enough among violent men, or as an alternative to *Christ!* when someone struck his thumb with a hammer. But the word was taboo for me. Four asterisks was all the law allowed in books at that time. Seeing them, I well knew what they stood for, but I never spoke the word aloud. To hear it from Jan was a shock; to hear it in relation to Pia was a greater shock. Jan went on, 'That's what I'd like to do to Pia — fuck her!'

He fell silent, sat on the edge of my bed, scowled. I said nothing. Jan got up and went to the window. After a while, in a very different voice, he said, 'The trouble is that Pia might even let me have her. She'd strip off everything except that slight, *unnerving* smile. And in memory of it afterwards, I'd cut my throat with a palette knife.' Jan grinned. He added, sadly, 'The only way I can ever have Pia is to paint her.' He gazed out of the window and was silent; dreaming, I supposed, of how he would paint Pia. The disturbing thought of her gave way to the challenges of art, of form, colour and composition. Jan was back on safe, familiar ground.

As I had sometimes looked to Alice's paintings to explain her, so I now looked to Pia's paintings to reveal the source of her extraordinary being. The paintings were plain to see, but what was it about them I could *not* see, yet sensed to be there? More quiet than I could find in myself seemed needed in order to enter them; one walked lightly in that lighted world, or not at all. But nothing was hidden; her secret was an open one. Her landscapes were clearly, recognizably, of the world all about, but lit by an awareness not only of the light on all things, but as well of a light *within* them. A small frog in the corner of one painting *glowed.* Yet it was an ordinary frog — if any frog, or indeed anything in this world, can be 'ordinary.' I looked at her painting of the hill that was to be seen out of the window. I looked out of the window at the hill. They were recognizably one and the same, and yet . . . Was her painted hill as the hill truly *was?* I could not see it so, and longed to see the world as Pia did, translucently.

Occasionally, Pia's landscapes showed human figures, but only and always in relation to the landscape, in proportion and in place as 'minute particulars;' somewhat in the way of the Chinese; not as so often in the west where man, as the measure of all things, stands large in the foreground with hills and valleys, the wide sky itself, there to affirm and inflate him. Clearly, Pia saw humankind as an aspect of Nature, as part of the Whole, not apart from the ground underfoot, the sky overhead, the small lark in that immeasurable sky.

Pia's paintings were without perspective, held together by some inexplicable balance to make a whole, but offering no fixed viewpoint to mark where the painter stood and to where, to whom, all the elements in the painting could be referred back. There was no painter, only the painting. Later, I happened upon another woman's wish *to see the landscape as it is when I am not there.*[24] Surely this was the way Pia saw the world.

Pia's colours were for the most part muted — great areas washed with shades of grey or of subtlest colour; then a sudden point or line or swirl of black, or a bead of bright red, of green, blue, yellow or gold. Entering such a painting, one walked, as it were, over the wide land under a wide sky in awareness of the unity of all things, of the Whole . . . and then stopped to go down on one's knees to see some 'minute particular' — a wild flower, a fly, a bee on a foxglove, drawn with meticulous care to show that for the moment of seeing, nothing existed in all the world but this one flower, this fly, this bee; each thing flowering, flying, bee-ing by its wild lone, in no way lonely; at home in the Universe.

I came also to see in this Pia's way of emerging out of the silence she inhabited to make a small gesture, speak a single word; only to return to stillness, to silence. But her movement and the stillness, her word and the silence were not opposing things. The bright flower was not apart from the space all about it; the black and golden bee was, as it were, a solid concentration of the same No-thing that, when diffuse, appeared as pale grey sky. This was art; this was also, I would learn, the findings of science; the actual nature of things, as far as words, as thoughts, could tell of it.

Above and beyond all, it was the 'ground' of Pia's paintings, as of herself — the empty places, the infinite space — that made for wonder. Painted in great detail and out of the closest observation, her fly could seem more 'real' than any ordinary fly; at least, as we ordinarily see it. This was within the bounds of the mind, or of the imagination: it could seem a matter of knowledge, of great skill. But what of those areas, whether painted or left unpainted, where there was nothing to be seen? How was Pia able to make that *nothingness* seem all as alive as the fly?

It was with awe, even with alarm, that I first heard Pia

tell of the *Nothingness* of things. Blaise Pascal once wrote that the contemplation of the *silence of infinite space* terrified him. I could understand this: I had walked at midnight alone on the moor. But Pia in silence and infinite space seemed in her element as a salmon in water, a gull in the air. So it was for all of us, she said: we could know ourselves as distinct beings, as unique things, only by the no-thingness, the space surrounding, containing, upholding all. Nothingness accompanied all things. She made an exercise of it. She put a chair on a desk and asked the class to draw only the *space* around the chair, between the slats of the back, around the seat, between the legs. Attending to nothing, drawing nothing, a chair appeared.

I had thought of nothingness as the absence of things. Pia showed it as Presence. But words are things, and cannot tell of nothingness without making 'something' of it. It is said that 'out of nothing, nothing comes.' Pia showed that out of No-thing, everything comes, and comes alive.

Many years after, I came upon a Chinese painter saying: *When the empty places are right, the whole body comes alive.* I said 'Pia!'

In the world as in quicksand some suffer to be so and long for another world, a Himalayan cave, or a high monastery or haven, a Heaven of some kind. Some long for another world that they sense is in this one; they suffer their blindness. Alice seemed of this kind. *Life is a paradise,* said Dostoievsky. *We are all in paradise but we don't see it . . . Nature is sinless . . . We don't understand that life is paradise, for we have only to understand and all will be fulfilled in all its beauty.*

Some, a few, may be so well aware of that other world in this one, that they can have no wish for anything but what is all about them all the while. For them, that other world is this one.

Pia was of this kind: an extraordinary being who did only ordinary things. It was extraordinary that she did not walk on water, rise into the air. 'Can you rise into the air?' someone asked Laotzu. Laotzu answered, 'I can refrain from rising into the air.'

Pia put her feet down firmly, no more than an inch above the earth. She got up in the morning and went to bed at night; between times she ate bread or whatever was given; drank water but welcomed wine when it was offered; she walked, talked when the need arose, touched, tasted, listened, looked, *saw.* Sometimes she painted what she saw. Tears filled her eyes sometimes; oftentimes she smiled. Things happened to her, through her. As the tree outside her window she responded to every weather. But she bore no scars. Nothing stayed beyond its time, so that at the end of each moment she came newly to the next. She left no trace, as a gull leaves no track in the sky, like the wind itself, like water flowing . . .

All my wondering about Pia only increases the wonder of her; only proves the lumpishness of thought, the opacity of words, of all my attempts to tell of her. I give up, fall silent, let go of her . . .

And at once: Pia is before me, whole and clear within me. Herself silent and scattered as ashes on the wind that took the leaves that last autumn of her life, she is at once *present:* near, dear, immediate, manifest — all the bread and wine of her, her unswerving look and little smile.

And in this light of Pia within me, I find myself smiling — a little smile.

An old Chinaman said: *When your work is done, withdraw. Such is the way of Heaven.* Hearing of Pia's 'untimely' death, I wept and smiled: 'Such is the way of Pia Malone.'

7 MAGDA

Damnation's a good girl. She loves me.
Christopher Fry

I PERSISTED IN FOLLY. THE NEXT SUMMER, AFTER ONLY nine months at Dartington, I left. It was not from discontent. The school had fulfilled its promise of adventure, only to make me eager for more. I admitted the need for further education, but of a kind that no school or university could offer. I wished to live dangerously.

'Meaning what?' asked Alice.

'Meaning London' I said. London would surely provide my next step into the world. Beyond the city of London lay Gauguin's green island in a cobalt sea, where brown women in red pareos walked on a golden beach; London was on the way to Chimborazo, Cotapaxi, Popocatepetl.

'What will you do in London?'

'I don't know, Alice. I want to earn my own living for a start. Anything will do until I know what I want to do.'

Alice gave me money enough for a month, took me to Taunton station. 'It is not that I want to go to London only to find a living; it's to find *life*' I seriously explained on the station platform. '*And* to find love' I added. Alice smiled. 'I mean I want to make love and all . . . I won't feel I've *begun* to live until then, until I've known a woman, like that French painter knew you, in the same way that you told me.'

Alice smiled. 'Send me a postcard sometimes, Michael. Let me know how you are, what you're doing. And come back whenever you want to — when you need to lick your wounds. London's . . .'

She did not say how London was. The train drew in. The guard called 'Paddington Train,' then named the stations along the way. I heard beyond: *Chimborazo . . . Cotopaxi . . . Popocatapetl . . .* The guard blew his whistle.

I went into Alice's arms. She held me a moment, then pushed me from her, said gruffly, 'Go now, Michael. And God go with you.' She wiped her eyes with her red spotted handkerchief, then held it high and waved it as the train pulled out. I was on my way to the Hesperides.

I wrote to Alice that evening: *I'm a bit scared, Alice, but, except you, nobody would know it. I took the straw out of my mouth and sauntered up the slope from the station like a pearl-buttoned cockney; made for the Park and found a room not far from it in Moscow Road, Bayswater. So here I am with night falling and I'm a bit scared as I said, and a lot excited. As you said, 'London's . . .' I'd say that at first sight London's full of women of all shapes and kinds and sizes and all* wanting *(I want to believe): and one of them somewhere (I want to believe) wanting just* my *shape, kind, size . . . I miss you, Alice, but won't let anyone see, anyone know — except you.*

That was the first of my notes to Alice, and longer than most. More often, I wrote briefly on the back of postcard reproductions of paintings that I knew she would enjoy. They were invariably bright, as the few words on the back tried to be. She would read between the blithe lines, while approving the absence of that self-pity to which I had been adolescently prone. 'Act *as if* you're brave' she once said, 'as you surely *are;* just as surely as you're scared. But it's no good acting as if you're scared. Act bravely.' Sometimes I would write letters to Alice in mind only, and heart: a way of whistling in the dark.

In the sleep of Somerset, London had seemed life itself; it was there that things *happened.* I found it true, but things seemed to happen without me. After the first excited days,

I knew a loneliness I had never encountered on the empty moor.

The one small window of my room looked onto a wall. I walked the streets late into the night or early hours of next day to ensure that on return I would at once fall asleep. If I had not wholly shed my shyness at Dartington, it had not mattered there. It returned now to plague me. Seven million people surrounded me. I dared not ask one: 'Please speak to me. I want nothing; just to speak with someone.'

My need was answered one night. I gazed into Hatchards window in Piccadilly. A man came and stood by my side. 'You like books?' he said. I turned and nodded. The man was elderly; grey hair showed under his bowler hat. He carried a stick with a silver handle. 'I have an absolute passion for books' said the man. 'Not just to read them but also to feel, to caress them, even to smell them gives me the keenest pleasure.' He smiled, 'Would you like to see my library?'

His flat was large, with a deep white carpet, and the main room lined with books, except where a painting hung, of a naked boy; and two drawings by Aubrey Beardsley. A man of as much wealth as of kindness — surely Lord Somebody-or-Other. While I looked among the shelves, the man went to make coffee. He returned in a dressing-gown of pale blue silk. We sat on a chesterfield of dark-red velvet. The man encouraged me to talk of myself. I told a little of my immediate past, confessed my present loneliness. The man put a thin, veined hand on my arm, said that he well understood: it was so with him also. He put his thin hand on my thigh. I was moved by the man's understanding, his sympathy, his affection.

Then the man began to talk of love, then of loving *me*. His calm kindly face distorted, his eyes enlarged, his breath came short and loud. I pressed back into the cushions. Suddenly the man was upon me, laying hands on me, seeking my mouth. Shocked, I lay still for a moment. Then hurled the man from me. He fell among cups and saucers, milk and sugar. Black coffee spilled onto the white carpet. The man lay still. Unconscious? Hurt? Killed?

My alarm grew. But then the man stirred, started to get up. I leapt up, made for the door. The man did nothing to stop me, said nothing. At the door, I turned to shout at the man, but he was on his knees. The agony in his face silenced me. I turned the key, opened the door, looked back again. Still on his knees, the man's hands now covered his face. I shut the door, ran down the stairs, hurried to my room.

The man had spoken of love. What manner of love was this? I raged through the streets, but by the time I had reached my room, the sense of outrage had gone. All that remained was the memory of a grey-haired old man, Lord Somebody-or-Other, on his knees, his hands over his face.

With no idea of what it involved, I applied for and got work in a City office with a grand name: Marine and General Mutual Life Assurance Company. I counted myself lucky so soon to have found the means to a living. At the end of the first day, I wondered what one who wished to live dangerously was doing in such a place.

I sat on a high stool at the end of a long desk that stretched across the room. Similar desks ranged one behind the other to the back. I answered the phone, went forward to the front counter to deal with or to redirect enquiries, put stamps on letters, ran small errands. It was only a beginning, I was assured. Promotion would follow faithful service.

The faithful sat on their high stools in their appointed places. They sorted and shuffled papers, bent over enormous ledgers, filled them with figures. Every now and then, one would dip his pen in red ink, take up a long round black ruler and draw a line across the page, signifying death. In due time, I was assured, I would move along the front desk to its end, then to the beginning of the second row, then along that row to work my way back and back as retirement or death took those ahead of me. At the end of the last row, I could hope one day to sit at the single separate desk of the Assistant Manager, and there dream of going beyond, through the door at the back to the Manager's office. The way was clear and certain. Meanwhile I could insure myself against sickness, accident, fire, theft, be endowed in my old age, and at the end die nobly in the knowledge that with a policy secure in the company's vault, I had deprived Death of its sting.

Sometimes I would be asked to go down into that windowless vault to bring up numbered policies, or one or more of the great leather-spined ledgers on a trolley in the lift. I would go down gladly, breathe deeply of the solitude and silence of the vault, take from under my coat a book that told of uninsured sailors in small unsafe ships on wide uncertain seas, of men who climbed mountains without a policy in their packs, to come upon life in the presence of likely death. I dreamed to do similarly, and the vision would sustain me after my return to the tomb above.

Some books did not help. *Ah! realize your youth while you have it,* I read. *Don't squander the gold of your days . . . Live! Live the wonderful life that is in you! Be always searching for new sensations. Be afraid of nothing.*[25] I had the passage by heart and silently repeated it over and over, biting my lip so that I would not scream at the sight of the faithful; at the knowledge that I could be counted among them.

My days were made possible by the presence of the single woman on the staff. On my first day, Miss Symonds smiled in welcome and, it seemed, held my moist hand longer than was needed. From that day on she smiled whenever I went to her. I loved her at once and for ever, but was shy and uncertain how to declare it. I said 'It's a nice day, Miss Symonds, isn't it?' Miss Symonds looked out of the window at the small rain and understood, the way women do. She smiled. 'Yes, I suppose it is. Why, yes! It *is* a nice day.'

She did not seem to mind the way I was: seventeen with spots, and shy. She did not mind when I made mistakes; she even hid them from others. If the world was perfect, what would women do? If men were wise and able as they pretend to be; if men were as angels indeed, as they were in words, Good Lord! what would women *do* with all the love that is in them, pressed down and spilling over?

'How's your cold today, Miss Symonds?'

Red-eyed, she sniffed, 'Mud bedder, Michael, dank you.' She did not want to upset me, to hurt me in any way.

Inevitably she did. She was unfaithful. I had already learned a little of the pain that accompanies love, so that I should not have been surprised when Miss Symonds came one day to the office with a diamond ring on the third finger of her left hand. Taking it like a 'Man,' I marked the occasion by giving her a bottle of scent called *Love in a Mist*. After a month she was gone for ever.

The woman who took her place was old; all of forty, married, fat, moustached, efficient, bossy. Who did she think she was to order me around so? I who in a dark wood had peered under a gypsy's skirt? who, in an attic, had seen a woman *all over,* the white of her *and* the black?

I tried hard to love Mrs. Brown as I knew St. Francis would have done — loving wolves as he did. I was reading a life of the little man of Assisi at the time, so that my dark suit was only an appearance — in truth I wore a long grey robe with a rope about the waist, as surely as in my socks and polished shoes I walked barefoot. In the lunch hour I sat upon a bench to read of the Saint and to eat my sandwiches. The sparrows came at once, recognizing me for what I was: another Innocent, a Fool of God, and so a figure of scorn in the godless city. After an hour, I returned to the office in a glow of goodwill, knowing no evil. Five or ten minutes later, depending on when Mrs. Brown called me, the vision faded. I heard only her brigadier voice; saw the black hairs on her upper lip.

For some weeks I stayed and suffered my inability to love Mrs. Brown; then gave notice. On the last day I ran laughing and free, all the way down Fenchurch Street.

Within two days I was washing dishes in a restaurant by Tottenham Court Road. I read of Brother Lawrence in the monastery kitchen practising the Presence of God among 'the pots and the pipkins' in the very midst of 'those mundane tasks' for which he had great aversion. I washed the greasy plates to the glory of God.

In time, delivered of this, I found work in a bookshop. It would serve for a living until I was ready to live out all the things of which I so avidly read.

I started to do so. Lacking one small girl to love, I planned to love the world; no less. Not being good, I needed to *do* good. But how and what? My inability to believe in a bearded God or in any abstract Spirit made impossible an old dream to be a country parson at Selbourne. Should I be a missionary of some sort, on a savage island, bringing no foreign God, but only the natives' own good? Or in darkest Africa, be a doctor, living among lepers, the lame, the halt, and the blind? Until the way showed, I planned in all spare hours to be a saint.

I went to live among the poor in the east end of London. I rented a high room in a grey terraced house. Throughout the day, the woman of the house shuffled about in slippers, a loose gown and hair curlers, a cigarette dangling from her lips. In the evening she came alive, removed the curlers, put on a gaudy dress and left the house on high heels in a cloud of cheap perfume; around her neck, a fox-fur that looked the worse for hounds. Behind her she left her child, a thin girl who slept in the room next to mine at the top of the house.

Awakened the first night by angry shouts, I hurried out of the room, leaned over the stair-rail to see the woman of the house, naked on the floor below, hurling abuse, bits of clothing and heavy boots after a naked man hurrying down the stairs. The woman went on shouting at the man as he dressed in the hall below. The woman's daughter stood at my side. I could see the thin neck, the bones of her spine above the line of her nightdress, her stick-like arms. She looked tubercular. The woman of the house was beyond my ability, but surely I could save her spindly daughter? How the child must suffer her circumstance, the immorality of her mother! When the girl straightened, however, she was smiling. The front door slammed. The mother disappeared, muttering. Her door shut. Still smiling, the girl shrugged her shoulders, turned back to her room.

Clearly, my first task was to fatten the girl. When her mother left each evening for the local pub, the girl came to my room to gulp down bread, butter and golden treacle, fruit, milk, chocolate and other foods I would buy on my way back from work in the evening. The woman of the house seemed well content with my assumption of responsibility for her child. I washed the girl's face and hands; brought books from the library to read to her; bought paper and paints for her; took her to a film sometimes, to the Tower of London, to the zoo.

It was all well and nobly done until the day I made a drawing of her. I had often drawn her as she played on the floor with the doll I had given her, or as she herself drew or painted, or read with her chin in her hands. Sometimes she posed for me, though able to be still only a short while.

She came one night in her nightdress, lay on my bed, joined her hands behind her head. I was reminded of Goya's painting of *The Maja Clothed*. Some small likeness in the pose apart, there could be little connection between the thin girl and that lusty mistress of the painter, except in my imagination — there, and in the girl's fixed stare, the waiting in her eyes, even (I could imagine) in their calling. But the child was restless, she shifted about, then got off the bed, went to my biscuit-tin, then back to her room. I stared at the drawing. Then, taking my cue from Goya, I rubbed out the girl's nightdress, gave full breasts to the figure, spread the hips, put flesh on the thighs, a smudge of hair where they met — Behold: *The Maja Naked!*

The drawing at the end resembled the girl only a little

but revealed much of me. For the first time I felt uneasy in my saintly role. The girl herself did nothing to uphold my ideal image of the relationship, seemed unaware of any need to be saved, oblivious of any wrong done to her by her dissolute mother, by her surrounds and circumstance. It was for her simply the way things were. She simply felt the pain they brought; found pleasure in them whenever she could; was quick to profit from them. She called 'Uncle' every stranger she found in the kitchen in the morning, rejoiced in the pennies and sweets that were her share of the spoils. Her mother's rare twinges of guilt also brought gifts. The child was well content.

I thought of her as a child, but in her face was already an omen of the woman she would become: it was alarmingly like her mother's face. The child's apparently knowing smile, the look in her eyes sometimes, made a child of me.

The mother had told me that her husband was away working. It was true, said her daughter; her father was doing 'hard labour.' I learned more of the man one evening when the girl climbed onto my lap. Her father was often away, she told me. When home, her father was often drunk. He never paid much attention to her, she said, except when he pulled her onto his lap to sit just as she sat on me. Her father would hold her as I was doing, she said, then pull off her pants, undo his flies and let his 'thing' rise between her thighs. He would then raise and lower her until he spent himself upon her. The child's account was casual, factual, unjudging, but I listened with growing horror and anger at her father. At the story's end, the child put her thin arms about my neck and lisped, 'You can do it if you like. You're not like my dad. You're nice.'

To my horror at the facts she told, I added my imagination: I *was* like her father now, not at all nice. I pushed the girl from me, got up. She stood bewildered before me. I could say nothing to answer her look. She shrugged her thin shoulders, took a biscuit from the tin, went. I turned and fell upon my bed in shame.

I was no saint, no saint at all.

The next morning I told the woman of the house that I would be leaving. Her daughter ran up the stairs after me, leaned back against the closed door, said over and over, 'You can't go. You *can't.* You *can't.* Just when I've found a friend . . . Don't you like me any more? What 'ave I done? You can't go. I'll *die* if you go.'

Later, in bed, I was reading in a mystical work of 'the game of Love which the Lord plays with His poor sinful creature' . . . The girl flung open the door, ran and threw herself across me. 'Please don't go away. *Please.* I'll die. I'll die.'

I put my arms about her. She lifted her head from my chest and looked at me in a way that belied her few years. I tried to remember St. John of the Cross, Nicholas da Cusa, Eckhardt and Suso. I failed. She is only a child, a child only, a *child,* I repeated, as some will cross themselves at the sound of thunder, at lightning in the night sky. The incantation had effect in the end. I grew still. I held the girl's head to me, patted her back, said to the child she once again was, 'I'll buy you a present before I go.'

The girl lifted her head. 'You will? Honest?'

I nodded. 'What would you like?'

'Chocks'

'I'll buy you a box of chocolates.'

'A *whole* box! Honest?'

'A whole box. Honest.' I kissed her brow, patted her shoulders. 'Go to bed now.' She went happily to bed. I lay back in relief.

The next evening I climbed the stairs to my room heavy with the realization of my inability to be a saint, even in spare hours. I took the crucifix off the wall above my bed, and *The Song of St. Francis* that I had lettered and hung nearby. I packed my clothes, my books — the lives of the saints, the sayings of mystics, a copy of *The Imitation of Christ* I had not yet read, and now knew that I would never read. Playing the saint had proved me a satyr.

I left the cases in the hall, went into the kitchen. I paid the woman of the house the full rent for the week that had only just begun. She put the notes into the top of her dress, between her breasts, smiled, 'Pity you're goin.' Been nice 'aving you. Maybe I'd 'ave posed for you too, now I know you better — in the *altogether,* maybe!' She laughed. Her daughter, behind her, stared at the box that I carried. I handed it to her. She took it to the table, sat down, tore off the wrapping, lifted the lid off the box, gasped to see row upon row of chocolates of all shapes and coloured wrappings. She took one. 'Strawberry!' she exclaimed. As she chewed it, she considered the next. 'Caramel!' she announced with her mouth full, her eye on another.

'Goodbye' I said. It was a solemn moment.

'Bye' said the girl without looking up. 'Ta for the chocks.'

I had hoped that the parting would not be *too* difficult. It was disappointingly easy. Surely the occasion called for a *little* drama — some rending of hair, a light beating of the breast, a small torrent of tears? Nothing happened. The woman of the house was now busy at the stove, her back to me. The clock ticked. The thin girl sat at the table with one arm embracing the box of chocolates, the bulge of a chocolate in her cheek, wholly absorbed by the problem of which one to eat next. I smiled at her. She was to have *died* at my going.

I smiled at myself. My good deeds had gone unnoticed. I was not the saint I supposed myself to be, while the thin girl was as I had always known her: despite all my noble intentions, bread, butter and golden treacle, she was as thin as ever, unwashed as ever, as ever unsaved and, it seemed, content to be so.

I turned away, picked up the cases, went out of the front door down the steps into the street, turned west.

Dear Alice, as you see, I have yet another address. You'll be glad to know that I gave up the insurance business. I washed dishes in the evening for a while and am now working in Foyle's bookshop. My last room in Whitechapel was at the top of a working-class house: the Man of the House was away working: hard labour. The Woman of the House swaggered out to work in the evenings, flourishing a moth-eaten fur and smelling of roses of Picardy. She often brought work home, and hard and noisy work it was sometimes. The Daughter of the House was too young to work, but she's a natural and is learning fast. I worked unnaturally hard at being better than I am, acting as if I was St. Francis, but the birds saw me at best as one of those old Popes with a love of pate-de-lark's-tongues and flew away at my coming, and the many wolves around there went on being wolves – being bad, that is; no better for my coming. The Daughter of the House learned nothing from me, but taught me that I must give up this saint-business.

I found a room in west London and began again. No longer under the strain of being a saint, I could now admit the sinner I was, I could allow those dreams I had denied or had regretted all the while I was being only 'good.' The glowing angelic girls of my day-dreams gave way to darker women: I dreamed of bawds, banshees, harpies, succubae.

Such nightly visitations were accompanied by an increasing awareness of women by day: their haunting *otherness,* their strange being, the alien loveliness that showed when my imagination lifted the clothes from them as they sat in public places or walked the streets ahead of me. I seemed to detect a woman-smell beyond any perfume a woman might put on. The sheer presence of the feminine! Simply to watch a small girl playing on the grass; to share a table in a cafe with a strange woman, saying nothing but simply being there beside her; to sit beside an old lady in a bus . . . all brought some access of virtue, of vice sometimes, of vitality always.

Dear Alice: In a pub this evening, near Covent Garden, living dangerously . . . A woman, not young, not young at all and stout as the Guinness in her fist, comes to my corner, sits and stares at me, significantly . . . *The enormous meat of her breasts! and her dress cut so low and her leaning over: only a bit more and I swear I'd see beyond, even to the hairs below, and they wouldn't be bright henna as her head. She pushes, but I don't fall,* can't . . . *am suddenly* very *vegetarian. Living dangerously, nevertheless, I buy her another pint. But then: I have to go, I say; to meet my girl, I say. She straightens at once and suddenly sober, says, 'I understand, my dear . . .' and puts her plump hand on my arm, gently, so gently. And I go from her, sad with lying to her; sad with no girl to go to, no girl at all . . . sad that there's no girl at all at all. I leave the pub, walk the streets in a cloud of self-pity until I stop, stand, see how much that fat old whore has to be sad about and is not sad or does not show it to the world, even forgets her own needs in face of the love I pretend to have for another, puts her hand on my arm, says she 'understands, my dear . . .' I see my sadness, self-pity, self. And, Enough! I say. There is no girl. So: there is no girl. So I must walk alone. So I* will *walk alone, walking by my wild lone, waving my wild tail . . .*

How much I have to learn, dear Alice, but how many are my teachers here in London town: thin young girls and fat old women, a man here and there, but invariably women in various guises, wise beyond the wise books I read all the while, the philosophies, the holy scriptures. Do you know The Cloud of Unknowing *by some anonymous medieval author? Have only dipped into it so far:* . . . the higher part of contemplation, as it may be had here, hangeth all wholly in this darkness as in this cloud of unknowing; with a loving stirring and a blind beholding of the naked being of God Himself only. *But I wonder: is there a kind of beholding that is not blind? A beholding which (itself being naked) sees the naked being, not of some medieval God, but of all that* is *here and now, a* Sun of Unknowing, *as sure as the sun above London town this morning unknowingly shining; its naked being shining, simply shining, Alice dear, dear Alice.*

Desire is the Devil's name; his time, place and playground is the seventeen-year-old body of a youth in the streets of London. So the black-suited Priest of my schoolboyhood told me.

We met in the Strand. We had walked towards one

another with dawning recognition — on my part with increasing unaccountable fear — until we stood opposite one another. 'It's Michael Adam, surely?' said Mister Sin. I shook the cold bony hand, surprised to find myself looking directly into the Priest's eyes. The Priest had always hovered over me, lean, hungry, vulturine. He looked even more lean now, more hungry, but he no longer hung over.

The Priest suggested coffee. I took him to a café where I often went to dream, draw, write. It was below street level and lit by red shaded lights. Mister Sin sat down and looked around to find what he sought: a scarlet woman alone in a far corner. A man sat at another table a little way from her. Clearly it was a place of assignation, of secret shadowed meetings.

The priest lit a cigarette, sucked in the smoke, blew it out, coughed his old cough, his shoulders shaking and bowed over the cave of his chest. Recovered, he asked 'What have you been doing, Michael, since I last saw you?'

A fear I had thought to have forgotten overwhelmed me. The Priest's question had reminded me of once-dread confessions.

I took a deep breath and told of my public school, and of Dartington. The Priest disapproved of that 'Godless place.' Defiantly, I said that I had been happy there. I then told of the Insurance office. The Priest approved of that. I said that I had been unhappy there. The Priest was alarmed to learn that I was now living alone in London.

The world is a wicked place, the Priest said, and of all this wicked world, London is the wickedest place. London was a City of Sin, concerned with the arousal of lust, the satisfaction of Desire. And if Desire was the Devil's name, his accomplice was Woman. The Priest spoke with knowledge, for he had heard about Soho, and had gone to see for himself. Brazen women walked the streets there, leaned out of windows calling endearments to men on the pavements below. One such woman had stood directly in the Priest's way, saying to him, 'Hullo, darling.' To *him!*

'Are you *shameless?*' he had thundered at her. 'Can't you see that I'm a man of God?' He had put his hand to his clerical collar. The woman had only smiled, 'You could be on holiday.'

I laughed. Mister Sin glowered. 'It's no laughing matter, Michael. And if you find that funny, I do right to fear for you.' He lit another cigarette from the butt of the first, frowned at his coffee, seeing some dark fate for me in the stained bed of a scarlet woman.

I said nothing. After a while the Priest reached out and picked up the book I had put down on the table: Francis Thompson's *The Hound of Heaven.* The Priest read a little, looked up in surprise, 'You're reading this?' I nodded. The Priest turned back to the book, read aloud:

I fled Him down the nights and down the days;
I fled Him down the arches of the years;
I fled Him down the labyrinthine ways
Of my own mind; and in the mist of tears
I hid from Him, and under running laughter.

Is this *your* story, Michael? The Priest spoke gently. I shrugged my shoulders. I was not going to confess anything to him anymore. The Priest read on:

All which I took from thee I did but take,
Not for thy harms,
But just that thou might'st seek it in My arms,
All which thy child's mistake
Fancies as lost, I have stored for thee at home:
Rise, clasp My hand, and come!

The Priest was more moved than I had ever known him to be. He lit another cigarette, had another bout of coughing, swallowed some coffee, ate some cake. Then, with more of a smile than I had ever seen on his face, said 'You know, Michael, I'd always hoped and prayed that you might one day be called.'

'Be called?'

'To be a priest of Holy Mother Church. I had high hopes for you. Even as a small boy you showed signs.'

I looked at the Priest's blotched sickly skin, his hollow cheeks, his bent shoulders, sunken chest. Was this the height of the Priest's hopes for me: to be as himself with his chain-smoking, his hacking cough, his stained fingers, his mourning dress? I looked away. I did not need to look or to listen to Mister Sin to know the misery of the man: how he waited upon death to release him from the burden of being alive; how he talked of God's love and of the love of God without ever having known love of any ordinary or awful kind, not even as much as Alice's ducks or that scarlet woman of the streets who had called to him, 'Hullo, darling,' to him who was *never* on holiday.

I turned back to the Priest. He was bent over the book again. How carefully he had arranged the thinning hair to hide his balding head; how blackly the bristles stuck out above the gaunt pale cheeks and the cut of his razor; how yellow his skin . . .

I was looking at the Priest with other eyes now; wishing only that I had the skill to paint the Priest as he was; without judgement, just as he was. I now saw that the long fingers of the Priest's right hand were of the yellow glaze of a plate from Provence; the blue binding of the small book held by those yellow fingers showed against the red-and-white squares of the table-cloth; his sleeve was black; his coffee-cup was brown, the spoon silver, the cakes multicoloured. And beyond all this was the background of the room with its shaded lights and shadows, with the woman at the table, the man alone, two lovers now hand-in-hand in a far corner, and the city up the stairs, and above the city, the sky, the sun in the sky, and there and here and everywhere the invisible Ground of Being of which the mystics told. If only I could have painted the Priest in that place, at that time; in his place, playing his part in the Whole. How well the man played the part of a miserable Priest; how *miserably,* and so how well.

My old fears had fallen away. I felt sad for Mister Sin, even a strange love. Tears came to my eyes. I wanted to tell the Priest that we should read no more of Heaven and its Hound; only *see* what was all about us, given us at that moment. And the grace of knowing — in the words of a woman of the Priest's own creed — how Sin was behovely. *And all shall be well, and all manner of thing shall be well.*[26] Not shall be . . . *is*.

I wanted to say many things, untellable things. I said nothing. Some inexplicable gladness had me by the throat.

The Priest looked up from the book, saw my eyes, said, 'Are you all right, boy?' Without waiting for an answer, he looked at his watch, put down the book, said it was time for him to go. Before going, however, he offered me hope. He told how God cared for those who had strayed; of Jesus and of the lone lost sheep; of Mary, our Lady of Mercy's continuing concern for sinners.

So: *that* was my trouble! I had done nothing really, committed no sin *worthy* of God's notice or of Our Lady's mercy. I was still a good boy; a white sheep, not worth saving. God was busy hounding after worthier men with bright fire in their eyes and grey smoke curling up from their trouser bottoms. Our Lady was where mercy was *earned*. My wrong was being right; virtue was my vice. And that simply was not sin enough to merit God's care or Our Lady's mercy.

I smiled, but said nothing of my new understanding. The Priest took my silence for consent. He blessed me, drew a cross in the air before me. The Priest called Our Lady Waitress. She came but the Priest saw none of her, nothing of her dark eyes, her raven hair, the swell of her breasts above him, her pumpkin belly, her hips, the whole harvest festival of her. He was busy checking the bill against the prices on the menu. He put down the exact amount, counting it out in small change from his purse. He pushed the plate towards Our Waitress without a glance at her.

I did more than glance. An old memory assured me that under her uniform, her breasts as she bent, swung away from her body like bells, fell back as she straightened, and when she turned her back and walked away, a lower, heavier bell tolled. No longer a saint, I could notice such things.

In the street at the top of the stairs, Mister Sin turned, looked sadly into my eyes, saw doom. He held out his hand. I took it in both of mine, smiled, 'Give my regards to Lough Gill, to the Isle of Innisfree; my love to the tinkers in the lane.'

Mister Sin did not smile. 'Remember what I've told you, Michael. London's no place for a man, let alone a young lad.'

'I'll find my way,' I assured him. The Priest shook his head, turned and walked away. I watched his black back vanish into the crowd: There by the grace of God go I; a part of me is a gloomy priest going his way, as surely as a part of me is a seventeen-year-old youth glad to see him go.

I remembered what the Priest had said: he had warned me of Soho. I therefore went to Soho. The women and the men there seemed a people of the sun, with Mediterranean memories, quick to laugh and curse, embrace and burst into song, all without the constraints of my education. The shop windows showed strange foods, black olives, dried octopus and squid, great circles of cheeses and wines whose names I had only to read aloud to find myself singing.

Walking those streets at night revived an old dream to walk by my wild lone all over the world; not to change the world but to be witness to it simply, so to step out of my accustomed skin, go beyond the limits of my mind.

Eating spaghetti and drinking *Chianti* in an Italian restaurant, I dreamed and danced with gypsies, dived for pearls in a warm sea, and in a cold land knelt to enter the igloos of Eskimos whose hospitality to strangers, I had read, included the loan of a soft wife in a sleeping bag. I strode among lianas and giant lizards in a South American forest, peered into the womb of Popocatapetl, sailed in all weathers on all seas, went ashore to drink a dark wine, to sing bawdy songs and bounce the taverner's daughter. I loved and lost and loved again and so stored for my old age a host of memories — the sight of Fujiyama through the blossoms of a cherry over the black head of a yellow girl; the sound of temple bells in high Tibet and the piping of an Aegean shepherd; the smell of oriental bazaars, burn of Indian curries and cool of sherberts sipped on a flat roof at midnight under a low Moroccan moon; the touch of rare stones, of desert sand, of silk and cotton on the bodies of swarthy women, of those bodies when stripped.

Wherever my dreams went, they came upon women. I did not need to dream on them only: as Mister Sin had said, they stood brazen under the street lamps, leaned out of windows, from darkened doorways, called, 'Darling . . .'

I stood one night against a wall in Swallow Street, a little from the bright core of Piccadilly Circus. A whore swayed into the narrow street, saw me, came to me, stopped before me, smiled, 'Hullo dear. Could you use a nice girl on a night like this? A girl like me?' She spread her arms to show herself, 'Nice and naughty?'

I wanted to run. I wanted to stay. I stayed but could say nothing. With a lazy smile, the woman came closer, fixed me to the wall with her hips. Her breasts steamed with cheap scent; mascara made her eyelashes into spider-legs. Her lips were smeared with blood. She was vampire, priestess, a barbaric princess. I feared her at first sight while knowing that I had worshipped her from the beginning of the world and would love her for ever and ever. Tears started in my eyes. Church and school were only two dark years away, so that I could not say Yes! While the need of her, of any evidence of humankindliness, however feigned, was too urgent to let me say No! and send her from me. My pain became clear to the woman; so did my few and virgin years. She drew back, put her hand on my chest, looked at me gently, said she was sorry, said 'Things are quiet tonight. I was just going to have a coffee. Like to join me?'

I thanked her. I walked fearfully at her side to the end of the small street, then stopped. Regent Street was lighted, peopled, wide. Cowed by education, I could not walk into the open at the side of a whore. Two paces ahead, the woman stopped, at once understood. 'I'll walk ahead' she said. 'You can follow to the café.'

I blushed at her words. Ashamed of my small courage, my great ingratitude, I ran forward saying, 'I'm sorry. I'm sorry. It's just that . . .' I took her arm boldly then, smiled at her smiling, crossed Piccadilly Circus with her to a cafe in

Lisle Street where the red women came between times of trolloping.

Walking the wide streets with a very apparent prostitute on my arm was a kind of beginning; a sure, however shy, gesture of defiance. To walk at the side of a gaudy whore was 'not done.' I was doing it. At school and since, I had been accused of dreaming. I had dreamed of walking with a whore. Now I was daring it, doing it. I was no longer only a dreamer.

After that introduction, I went often to the café for the warm company it offered. After the first attempts, the whores did not embarass me with invitations. I had no fine will to refuse but, even if I had the cash, I had not the courage of my curiosity, of my want. I had also looked up *Syphilis* in a book with coloured illustrations. The women let slip their profession and let me be. Perhaps they were surprised by my innocence, by such faith as mine that could even see *them* innocent, even clothe them with the sun. Perhaps they were amused by it; perhaps made wistful. They were invariably kind.

Stalking on highest heels and overburdening the black satin dress she wore, a woman with ginger hair came to my corner one night and asked my name. 'My name's Margaret' she said in turn. 'But my friends call me Pat, or Mag. So it's Pat' she said, easing off her shoes and smiling. 'Or Mag.'

Short for Magdalene, I thought. I called her Magda from that time on. She was buxom, in all ways ample. In another age she would have made an orange girl for a cavalier king. All that was man in me suffered the sight of her on summer nights. After a while of knowing her it was certain that I loved her. In the light of the dark I then pursued, it seemed well that the coming of love and my entry into the world should be at the hands and hips of a whore. To Kipling's list of necessary virtues and qualifications, I had come to add the essential grace of knowing Woman. Magda's experience would undo my innocence, would make a

'Man' of me.

With the price in my pocket, I asked Magda for her body. She looked at me long and seriously before saying that we were friends, so that there could be no business between us. 'You can have me for the asking, Michael. But I ask you not to ask me.' She put her hand on mine.

I could have her! I had only to ask it. The wonder of it! But then I knew that I could not ask it. The sadness of it! Any man could have her, but not I. Don't you *love* anyone, Magda? I mean, not just make love to a man when he pays you.'

'I love no man' said Magda. After a long pause she went on, 'I loved a man once. I was nineteen and it was to be for ever. He didn't love his wife, he said; he loved only me and for ever and ever. But he stayed with his wife in the end and forgot me. All that was for ever was my memory of him. I can't forget him.' Again she paused before going on, 'After a long while I loved another man. He wasn't married, so that I thought *we* would be, and it would be for ever, as he said. I found that he was running after other women all the while. And that wasn't the worst of it: unable to trust himself, he couldn't trust me. With no cause at all, he was insanely jealous. When he hit me, I left him. I'd like to forget him. There have been many men since, but no man that I love. I love Rosemary.'

I knew the small black-haired whore, half Magda's age, who came to her in the street sometimes, to her table in the café always, to her flat often. They were good friends, I realized, but . . . 'But that's different' I said. 'Rosemary's a woman.'

Magda smiled. 'She's a woman, so it's different, of course. But you asked me if I loved anyone. I told you: I love Rosemary.'

'I meant loving *and* making love.'

'That's what *I* meant, Michael.'

Would I ever learn about love? The bounds of my understanding were repeatedly broken. I would enlarge the circle of my understanding to include new findings, new facts . . . only to have *that* circle broken, and I would stare into a world without limits of any kind that I could name 'love.' That unbounded world at once alarmed and called me.

I remembered that man who had spoken to me of love. In a world graced by women, it was incomprehensible that a man could want another man, one of his own kind; but that anyone, man or woman, would want a woman was well within my imagination. From where I sat in Magda's flat, I could see through an open door Magda's wide bed. Now I saw a ginger head on the pillow beside a black head; Magda's pale and ample body entwined with Rosemary's slim and dusky one. I was warmed by the sight. I smiled at Magda, 'I'm sorry. I didn't know about Rosemary. I don't seem to know *anything* about love.'

'You will, Michael. You will. You'll find a girl sometime. Not my kind, but someone you can go to bed with and wake up with, and not feel sad or sorry after; and you'll have breakfast with her and walk in the park with her and . . . well, *everything;* not just bed. There's more to a man and a woman than just bed, however lovely that can be. Believe me, Michael, that girl's worth waiting for.' She sat back and lit a cigarette before quietly saying 'The love of another woman is not what I want, Michael. I want a man as you want a woman, but I'm a lot older, perhaps a little wiser, so that I've learned to be glad with what I'm given — little things, like small Rosemary; knowing well that she loves me only a little, and will someday leave me.'

Years after, I could summon up the scent that Magda used; the smell of her room that varied a little with the flowers that were there; the smell of the toast that we browned before her gas fire on Sunday afternoons. I could see the shapes of the stains on the backs of two pictures that she turned to the wall on my first visit to her; and the pictures themselves when later she let me look at them. In a red woollen dressing-gown upon a wicker chair, she talked of many things, but mostly of love or the lack of it, of the ways of men and women, and of women of her own kind who were good and bad, as everyone else; no better, no worse; if even sadder than most. I came to Magda full of dangerous dreams and ideals that had root in that first sight of a stripped girl in an attic. I was gauche and eager to make a grail of any and every girl; to make of Magda a Saint Magdalene. She exposed my shallow faith but, fondly, gently, so that a deeper understanding could follow; one in which there was no less regard for women but even an increase of it, better founded on the firm dark soil of facts. Under her tutelage and care, I emerged, still innocent of experience, but no longer uninformed.

What I learned from Magda and from my own findings in those shadowed streets did not make life easier, for I gained no knowledge of the world without knowledge of myself. I was less able to distinguish the world without from the world within me — it was not flattering. Those who lived in Soho might seem of the sun, but those who came to it at night were for the most part solemn desperate men. Magda once said, 'Men come to me because they don't know how to love, so that I never have lovers, only sad or sick men; sad *and* sick for want of love.'

I saw men staring into windows that showed magazine covers calculated to inflame and stir up wants of many kinds. I stood beside a man one night: pale and thin, he seemed transfixed by what he saw, a rabbit before a snake. A sick man, surely. But as I drew back to walk away, I saw another reflection in the same window into which the man stared — my own.

The drive of men's desires seemed so dark, so dread and overwhelming, that I could believe they arose from some deeper level than the body's animal lust, out of some deeper longing. Were these men, was I in this desperate way looking for a lost rib, for that Eve of the original Adam? for Wholeness? Perhaps lust was not opposed to love, since love opposed nothing. But was lust *alone* a lack of daring?

— taking a woman's parts because it dare not take her whole: Beauty *and* Beast, the entire awe-ful beauty of woman *as she is,* even beyond her own knowing?

I found a magazine behind the cushions on Magda's sofa. I put it under my coat and took it home. At first I turned the pages in shock and excitement, but then more deeply, gently, was moved 'to the very bowels' by the sheer loveliness, the sensual wonder of woman's bodies. Then, surprisingly, I found that the displayed women who moved me most, did so by the look on their *faces,* by their eyes above all. What was it in a woman's look that could stir me more than all the exposure of her body, disturbing not my body only, but *all* of me?

The magazine told of other things beyond my understanding. I could admit to natural lust, was happy to be as the beasts of the fields in this. I was in awe and wonder of the sight of women's bodies, in part or whole, but what was this talk of whips? of chains? of inflicting pain? How, with the want of women, could there be cheap cruel wit at their expense?

I took the magazine back to Magda, saying that I was sorry to have taken it without her knowledge. She shrugged her shoulders. I asked her of these other things. The want of a woman was one thing, whether in lust or in love, but how could a man wish to hurt a woman? and himself wish to be hurt by her? I told how, in reading of such things, as in wandering the streets of Soho by night, I would sometimes feel the pavements give way under me, turn to soft black mud, a bog, a quicksand that could suck me down.

Magda's alarmed eyes filled with tears. 'Men are . . .' she began. Then went on, 'But how should I know how men are? Most whores hate men. Sometimes that's why they become whores, and those who whore for other reasons soon come to hate men. No wonder. Money apart, men give them nothing; men come to whores only to get, or to get rid of something, of their sick selves. But perhaps we all do that.' She added, 'Whores hate themselves.'

Magda, laughing in all weathers, offering warmth on winter streets, or in a daffodil dress between spring showers, or lush as summer, or as an autumn orchard, bountiful, offering her apples . . . Magda bantering solemn men as they went by, bartering her soft body when some man stopped, going gaily with him, swaying, smiling . . . Magda dreaming of the shop she would one day own in a respectable suburb when she was too old for the game, but playing her disreputable part disreputably meanwhile, to the best of her ability, unwithholdingly, with laughter always . . . Magda, uncomplaining of rain or fog or snow, of the abuse of men or of the bruises she sometimes bore. Everything could be laughed at, herself above all . . . Magda, the lively centre of any circle she entered; strong support of anyone in distress . . . Magda, herself a little sad sometimes, but only sometimes, and only a little . . . But Magda now: Magda at this moment *overwhelmed* . . . Magda *alone* . . . Magda *lost* . . . Magda *sobbing!*

Shocked, I could find nothing to say, could only reach out to Magda, put my hand on hers. After a while, Magda grew still, wiped her eyes, looked at me long; then whispered, 'You must go away from here, Michael. Promise me, please, that you'll go away from here. Come back sometimes to see me if you want to; come and go, but don't hang around here at night; don't *stay* here.' She spoke louder: 'You have to know such things, but only in order to cope, not to be taken in . . .' Even more loudly: 'Dear God! not to have the pavements turn to *soft mud! Promise* me, you'll go, Michael.'

'I promise.'

Magda smiled again. 'That girl we spoke of, remember? You'll not find her here.'

Although I would return sometimes on Sunday afternoons to see Magda, I went from Soho and found a room in Notting Hill Gate, not far from Kensington Gardens. I had turned into an owl, living by night. I became a lark again; was up early each morning to walk among trees and water. I breathed deep and slow and the desperation went from me. The old longing for the coming of love assumed, with Magda's help, a gentler shape. Now I wanted a girl with whom I could go to bed and wake beside, walk with in the park and everything; not even having to go to bed with her, not that only. I was prepared to wait upon her coming.

Much had happened in those months in Soho. Counter to my dreams had been the curse of shyness. Alone in the dark of my room, I was a Don Juan, a rare devil of a man; but met by the morning-after of any woman, my face would crimson, my hands grow hot and wet and enormous. I tried auto-suggestion, deep breathing, spinach and self-analysis; and when the advertisements assured me that I had only to measure forty-eight inches around the chest to have women wade out of the sea and surround me on golden sands, I drank more milk and took up weight-lifting.

Such things availed a little, but nothing helped so much as the whores of Soho. A little while after that first encounter and my visits to the Lisle Street cafe, I had only to walk within a certain area to find myself warmly, intimately greeted. I took confidence from the fact that I was on terms of friendship with women whom most men could only fear or condemn, only abuse or hurry by.

In those months I came to see how much in me had been feared or condemned at the bidding of the Priest and of others; how much had been abused or hurried by, hidden away or hidden from. I could no longer hide, nor wished to do so. Darkness was not the description of a country where I could choose to wander and could leave at will; it was half of me. I left Soho, but from that time on, walked by my wild lone in increasing awareness of my shadow. My shadow was not something I cast; certainly not something I could cast aside; it came with me, went with me always, everywhere, together with whatever there was of light in me. It was not a matter of denying the Light, but of bringing

to it Darkness, its bride.

I longed for the coming of love as a winter creature for the light of the sun, but sometimes, as I had told Magda, I felt only the overwhelming darkness of love and of the world about me, as of that in me. But I had come to see the impossibility of running from my shadow, of seeking to disown it, of turning my back on darkness. I learned instead to stand when threatened, to be still and say: *This darkness I acknowledge mine.*[27] I would repeat the words over and over until they came true and, miraculously, I would find myself enfolded by a peace that passed any understanding I could have of love, the dark or the light of it. The more I learned about love, the less I understood. But that lack of understanding, as the lack of love itself, was also a darkness that I could now acknowledge mine, as a bride, taken in sickness as in health.

8 SALLY

The honey of heaven may or may not come,
But that of earth both comes and goes at once.
Wallace Stevens

HER NAME WAS SALLY VAN DE VELDE OPPENHEIMER. *Swans in the winter air / A white perfection have.*[28] I called her Sally-O.

With her head high she sailed across the room, her breasts thrust forward — the figurehead of a ship, a swan in winter air, in summer water . . . in all seasons and every weather, a girl to be with: by night to sleep with, by dawnlight wake beside; in the bright of day to walk with, talk with, be still, be silent beside, in all ways be with.

I had waited for such a girl. I dreamed, and when I happened upon a nude by Modigliani my dreams took shape from it: I walked the streets, whittling down the women of London to my want of a girl with sloping shoulders, almonds for eyes, moon breasts, the neck of a goose. Here and there I came upon one who required only the minimum work of my imagination, but I blushed at the point of encounter; the bold bawdy words were not spoken. If I painted, would some eager woman come to my side? If I wore corduroy trousers and leather sandals, let my hair be brushed only by the wind?

Each evening after work I exchanged my old school tie for a loose scarf, took to drinking wine on the left bank of Old Compton Street and, emboldened by ignorance, bought charcoal and rolls of paper for the creation of life-size nudes. No less. One day in a café after a little pasta and overmuch wine, I drew upon the tablecloth and waited. But only the proprietress came, and she for the wrong reason.

One evening I put on a suit to go to the birthday party of a friend. A girl stood in the centre of a circle of men, and clearly delighted to do so. I did not join them but looked long and longingly at the girl — her high white breasts, her upright head, her hair golden as Troy, the sensual turn of her shoulders as she attended to one man, then to another. Even when, being spoken to, I had my back to her, I listened to that girl only, heard her laughter above all the clamour of the crowded room. She was at ease in such company as I could never be. But I had learned not to try, not to care overmuch, no longer to make wide wooden gestures, going to great pains to prove myself at ease. I sat still or stood still, sipped wine, talked when I was talked to, but only then. As always when I felt lost in a crowd, I sailed away, dragged my boat up on a bare silent beach where a brown, broad-nosed woman with an ancient smile lay waiting, her arms, her legs wide in welcome. Or was she white? as a swan in winter air?

To my surprise, but in the way of dreams, the girl came true, came to my side, saying 'I'm Sally Oppenheimer. You've been staring at me all evening. Why?'

I took a deep breath, dared to say 'You're very lovely.'

'That's what they all say. But they come and say it. Why didn't *you*?'

'So many seemed to be saying it.'

'But not *you*. That's why I've come to you. Is that your technique? To stand and stare at women and so make them come to you?'

She was smiling, bantering, bold. I was glad of that. A shy girl might have awakened my old shyness. When the girl said that she lived nearby, I asked if, at the party's end, I might see her home.

'Sure, why not?' she said. Another man approached her. I left them, well content to wait on the side until my time came.

But I looked at the girl with even greater interest now: she was a girl I would go to bed with. She had a way with men, was clearly a woman of experience. Having so long suffered my innocence, it was a woman of experience I wanted.

Sally made it all so easy. When I went to claim her at the party's end, she smiled as though we had known one another a long time, and she admitted my claim on her. I took her hand. On the way down Brompton Road I learned that she was South African; that she had just completed her education with some years at the Monkey School in London and at a finishing school in Switzerland.

'The Monkey School?'

'That's what it's known as because of its motto; same as the Three Wise Monkeys: *See no evil. Speak no evil. Hear no evil.*'

A fitting education for one who must return to South Africa. But I did not say it for fear of spoiling the night. There was only a little time left before she would leave England. Her parents, now on the continent, would shortly return to England, and they would all leave on New Year's Day. Only a month was left; so little time for 'everything.' But a month by my reckoning added up to thirty-one nights of love. I reckoned also by Sally's manner: the way of her hand curling and uncurling in mine; the look of her eyes when she turned to me, smiling all the while.

That night, however, had to be subtracted from the total. I had hoped to enter her home, her room, her bed, herself. But she was staying with an aunt who kept an eye on her in accordance with her parents' instructions. Her parents were puritanical, Sally explained. 'That's why they sent me to the Monkey School. If only they knew what I learned there! Evil — meaning *sex* — was what we cared most to see, speak and hear about much of the time.'

Sally seemed eager for 'evil.' When I stood before her on the steps of her aunt's house, she smiled unequivocally, so that I took her in my arms. She pressed hard against me, moved her hips. As I had been taught long ago, I pushed my tongue into her mouth. 'Oh, my god!' she cried. 'I want you. I *want* you. You must go!'

I understood: it was not the time; it was not the place. 'Goodnight, Sally-O' I said gaily, and went home knowing that at long last I would come to love, not on a far-away beach but on my own bed to which Sally would come in all her white perfection.

The time and place, however, were not easy to arrange. Except on special occasions such as that party where we had met, Sally — though nineteen, educated and 'finished' — was not allowed out late and alone with any man. In view of her spirited passionate nature, I was surprised that she should so readily take orders from her aunt. But her aunt took orders from Sally's parents who were, Sally made clear, tyrannical.

Such pressures apart, Sally herself showed a reluctance to go to my room that was inexplicable in the light of her embraces, the way of her hands under tables in cafe's and coffee houses. So little time was allowed us in the evening; and she wanted to see so much, she said; do so much before her parents returned and she must forever leave for the Cape. The next six evenings of the thirty-one nights that I had counted upon were spent exploring the bright streets and the dark lanes I knew so well. We saw much, did much, did everything one way or another, as Magda had foretold — everything but bed together.

On the seventh evening, for the first time, Sally came to my room. We had wandered at her request through the streets of Soho, had dined there and walked on afterwards. Sally looked at every whore on every corner. 'How *awful* that women should sell their bodies,' she said. I said nothing. 'That's *really* evil' she said. I said nothing. 'That woman smiled at you,' said Sally, 'as though she *knew* you.' I said nothing; allowing her to assume that I was a man of some experience.

For all her moral comments, the walk through Soho seemed to soften Sally. She agreed to go to my room. There she encouraged me to take all the liberties that her woollen dress allowed, but would not remove that dress. It was the place, she agreed, but not the time. She put her hand between my thighs, said she wanted me all as much, but there was not the time. Her aunt would be waiting.

'I'd like to be a prostitute' said Sally, as we were about to leave, 'for a night or two.' She leaned her shoulders back against the door, thrust her hips forward, smiled 'Think I'd make a good whore?'

'You'll have to take off that dress if I'm to answer that.' I was not smiling. Sally's smile left her. She pushed abruptly away from the door, stood upright, straightened her dress, looked at her watch, said we must go.

I saw her home. On the steps of her aunt's house, Sally was again bold. She probed my mouth with her tongue, rubbed against me like a cat, put her hand between my thighs; again said Oh! how she wanted me, then said I must go, she must go.

I said 'Goodnight, Sally-O.' It was all I could say.

I had learned to say nothing, to bite my lip into silence. I had never known anyone (unless myself) with sex so much in mind. Of late, I had only met whores. Sally told jokes that had been part of her education. I did not find them funny. Was I a prude? a puritan at heart? I could admit the sinner in me, the would-be satyr; could I acknowledge the puritan?

I learned to be silent over other matters. One day a negress walked ahead of us. I said 'Look! She sways like a willow; for all her coat and hat and high heels, she's still barefoot in the jungle grass, a jar balanced on her head.'

'You mean you *like* her?'

'But of course. Don't you?'

The negress turned the corner. Sally was a long while silent, then said, 'That black woman — would you sleep with her?'

'Gladly, if I knew her, as I know you; if I felt for her, loved her, as I love you.'

'You're all the same, you men,' said Sally, 'wherever you are. *Any* woman will do. Back home white men go with black women; over the border if they can't do it nearer home. I *know*. Ben, my brother — he's in the police — he's told me of places he's raided, places he's been to or knows about. And other things. He has even — promise not to tell? — he's even been with black women himself, before he was in the police; at least I suppose it was. But that was different: he treated them like . . . like black women. And anyway, they were just whores or girls he found wandering in the countryside whom he didn't have to pay. But you . . . you say you'd not only sleep with a black woman; you'd even feel for her, fall for her, even *love* her, for God's sake!'

Instead of answering, I asked, 'What if a black man in South Africa makes love to a white woman — with her consent, I mean?'

'She wouldn't consent. And if she did, that would still be the end of the black man. He'd be locked up or hanged.

'That doesn't disturb you, Sally?'

'It's different there,' she said. 'You can't understand how it is there. Here you see one black woman in the street, all dressed up — an actress or something — and she seems lovely in her black way. I suppose she is, *here;* if you like that sort of thing. But there you see *millions* of them, and you know that if they're not kept in their place, they'll rise up one day and swamp the whites, kill and rape and all.'

'One day they'll rise up, surely' I said. But I said no more. I was, as she implied, an ineffectual angel in an old school tie, seeing a single black woman and seeing her at worst as a welcome threat to my loins, not to my life.

I was silent; sad for the world, for Sally and me, for all women and men, black and white; for a South Africa that was not so much a place as a state of mind, available to everyone everywhere. Weep! Weep for us one and all. Weep for black women and white rapists; for white women and black rapists. Weep for Spain and bloody Franco, for Catholics and for Communists, bulls and bullfighters, wounded birds and small boys with catapults. Weep for widows in over-wide beds; for those in narrow beds who lie alone, never having known otherwise — meaning me. Weep for Sally and Michael in love, yet estranged by alien ways of life and attitudes; constrained by states of mind imposed by parents, priests, teachers, all the while their bodies bid them to be simple, to love one another while they could in the little time left before they must part, before they must die.

Although that first week had not brought Sally and me to bed, it had brought us closer in other ways. We spoke of love for one another, in streets and cafés, in the dark of doorways where we paused to embrace; and always and at length on her doorstep before she disappeared. Sally stopped playing the part of a woman of the world. The sly jokes ceased.

We walked often in the park, sat on benches when the winter sun came out, held hands at the theatre, in the cinema. The urgency went from me. In its own way and time, love was moving to its appointed end. We would come to make love as the natural, inevitable expression of the love that enfolded us. Everything Sally said assured it. It was simply a matter of time and place.

But then, a week earlier than expected, Sally's parents came. They now planned to see more of England before leaving for the Cape. I met them. Sally's mother was an upright handsome amazon; her body and her mind both corseted. Sally's father had been handsome once but, uncorseted, his belly strained the buttons of his coat, his red neck swelled above his impeccable collar. They were not impressed by me either. I could not claim to have been a determining factor, but after the meeting it was ruled that Sally would go with them on their tour of England. Thirty-one nights of love, already reduced to twenty-one, were now to have fourteen more taken from their total.

Sally and her parents returned to London less than a week before they were due to sail for South Africa. All that while, Sally was kept on a tight leash.

I was allowed to see her each evening, but for a short while only. Sally seemed cowed, her bright spirit dimmed.

But *one* night was allowed us, she gladly announced. Although it was their last night in London, her parents had agreed to let Sally go with me to friends known to them. She did not have to be home until half-past twelve, after seeing the New Year in.

Thirty-one nights of love had come down to one. So be it. Love would come on the last night of the old year and I would go newly into the next, a 'Man' at least. One night was one night. I also had learned to be glad for what was given — little things, like Sally for some small part of a single night.

We went to the party and, after only half an hour, left for my room.

I had worked on the room, especially on the corner where the bed waited. On the wall above the pillows blazed Van Gogh's *Starry Night,* not still and holy, but impassioned with swirling stars, a spinning moon, phallic cypresses. Alongside the bed was Rousseau's *Dream* of a pale woman on a jungle sofa listening to a dark man playing a yellow flute, all the while a lion glared among great leaves and giant flowers. Sally would surely hear the roar of that lion; the screech of brilliant parrots in the room. Beside that dream, Gauguin's women sat brown and wondering, or stood upright in orange light asking: *Whence do we come? What are we? Where do we go?* A small woodcut by the same Gauguin promised: *Love and you will be happy.* Around and about these prints were my own nudes in the manner of Modigliani; they implied experience, a knowledge of nakedness.

I had warmed the room all afternoon. I lit the gas fire again. In its glow stood a small round table with a red-checkered cloth; on it was an old *Chianti* bottle with a dripping yellow candle, a long baguette of French bread, black olives from Greece, Emmenthaler and Brie cheese, a fruity German wine left all night on the window sill to chill.

I took Sally's coat from her shoulders. It was of fur, but I said nothing. I expected her to exclaim at the sight of the room, but she said nothing; she seemed preoccupied. I poured the wine. *'Liebfraumilch'* I said, showing the label: 'The Virgin's Milk.' Sally did not smile. I raised my glass: 'To us, Sally-O; here at last and at last alone.' Sally did not sip the wine; she gulped it down; held out her glass for more.

I broke the long bread, cut the cheese. We ate by candlelight, emptied the bottle of wine. Sally was smiling at last, a little. I opened another bottle: a rich red wine.

After the meal, I sat down in a large chair by the fire. I held out my arms. Sally came, a little unsteadily but willingly enough. She sat on my lap. I ran my hands over her and, when she sighed, I undid the buttons of her dress. She lifted a little and I pulled the dress from her; she lifted again and I pulled the long petticoat over her head. She got up then, stood in a short vest and long stockings, took the clips from her hair. She was smiling. Smiling, she peeled off the stockings. I went to her, held her, then took the vest from her, uncovered her breasts; stared in awe of them a moment, then started to uncover her hips. Sally stiffened, held my hand, stopped me. I fondled her more, calling 'Sally, Sally-O,' until she moaned and made no further protest.

Sally naked! The fire lit one side of her with a steady golden glow; the candle flecked the other side with light and shifting shadows. Oh, Sally, Sally, Sally-O!

I lifted her up and carried her to the narrow divan. I had heard that the belly of a girl makes the softest bed. It was true. For the first time in all my days and nights, I lay naked along the length of a girl all as naked.

I had come far from that early beginning in an Irish wood with the tinker's daughter. So far, but no further: Sally lay

under me with her legs together, locked by the ankles, one over the other. 'Sally, Sally . . .' I begged.

'I can't, Michael. I can't . . . I *can't.*' She turned her head away, whispered to the wall, 'I . . . I'm . . . I'm a virgin, Michael . . . I'm frightened . . . I . . . I must keep myself for my husband.'

The shadow of her parents reached across London all the way from South Kensington to Notting Hill Gate. Sally was biting her knuckles. She was crying.

What could I do? What could I say but say, 'I'm sorry, Sally. I didn't know. I thought . . .'

'I pretended . . . like I pretend about everything.'

'Well, it seems to be all we're able to do. I've never had a girl. I thought you'd be the first. I thought . . . But it doesn't matter what I thought.'

'Oh, but it does, it *does.* I don't want to be a virgin, Michael. I want to be a woman. I want *you,* Michael, as much as you want me, but I can't, somehow. I just can't. I'm frightened and . . . Oh, I don't know . . .' She shook her head from side to side.

Thirty-one nights of love had come down to one, and that one night had come to this. But Sally was crying again. I gave up. I lifted off her, lay still at her side. She was crying louder now. 'Don't cry, Sally-O. Don't cry. Or, cry for us both. But don't worry. Don't be frightened. I won't do anything, I won't ask any more than you're able to give, than you've already given. I promise.'

I lay still, looking on her nakedness, hearing her cry. The bright lust leaked away, to be replaced by fondness and by philosophy. I ceased to complain of what I could not have, counted my blessings. I had, after all, lain upon a naked girl. It was another step towards the eventual coming of love. The rest would follow in its own good time, upon the coming of another girl, another time. Sally had stripped for me. That was something; it was much; coming from her, it was very much. 'Don't cry any more, Sally-O. Don't be afraid. I won't enter you. I promise.' I kissed her wet cheeks, her mouth, held her breast but only lightly; lightly stroked all the length of her body, looking on it now as from a distance.

After some while, Sally surprised me, saying, 'Michael, lie on me again, please. *Please.*'

I lay on her again. With no distance between us now, desire flooded back over me, over her — now that she knew she was safe. She moved under me, lifted up to me. Now that I no longer urged, no longer insisted on it, she opened her legs. I lay between them.

Now that I asked nothing of her, she raised her knees, spread her thighs, saying over and over how much she loved me; how much she wanted me. How near I was to the coming of love, how *near* — held from it by a word, a promise. I moved on her, over her, all but in her. Sally stopped saying anything that sounded more than animal, seemed lost in some dream of her senses. She was without words but her body all the while seemed to be saying *Yes! Yes!* Would she protest now if I entered her? Would she even *notice* if I entered her? I did everything, everything but enter her.

Suddenly, revellers were singing *Auld Lang Syne* in the street below us. Sally's eyes opened wide in surprise, bewilderment, pain. She had been wrenched out of a dream, suddenly lifted from that deep sensual sea to which she had at last given herself so wholly, unwithholdingly; into which she had sunk, and had wished to drown in. 'Michael . . . Michael . . .' she moaned, holding me fast to her with arms and legs, with all of her. But then alarm seized her, stiffened her body. 'I must go. They'll be waiting for me. Oh, forgive me, Michael. I must go. I must go!'

She got off the bed. I lay back and looked my last on her loveliness, on the veiling of her nakedness: the white cloth over her golden bush, her breasts covered and confined, the stockings pulled over her long legs and fastened to a belt; her petticoat then shielded most of what remained of her, then her dress hid the rest. I got off the bed, put on my clothes, held her coat for her, opened the door, looked back a moment on the place that was to have seen the coming of love. I managed to smile a little . . . a little.

Not much was said on the way back to her house, nothing that mattered. I had my arm about Sally all the way. The lights were on in the house. 'I knew they'd wait up for me' she said unhappily. I kissed Sally, tasted the salty tears.

'Oh, forgive me, Michael, forgive me . . . It was cruel of me. I . . .I . . . Oh, forgive me if you can. Now I'll never see you again, never, *never!* Goodbye, my darling. My darling, goodbye . . .' She turned her key in the lock and went in. I heard Sally's mother shout. The door closed.

'Goodbye, Sally-O.' I spoke to the door.

That moment at her door was to have been the sad but happy ending of the story of the coming of love. Love was to have come on that last night of the year and of our being together. We would have made naked love for the first and last time in the earliest hours of the new year and been glad for it; then said goodbye, and been sad for that. Glad and sad, we would have left one another on the doorstep where we had first embraced a month ago, a life, a love ago . . . glad and sad and grateful for what was given.

Alone in my bed again, I lay awake, haunted by Sally's eyes at the end, by the story's unhappy ending. In the morning I went to Victoria station to tell Sally that I was only grateful for all that had been, in spitc of all that had not been, to say, 'Goodbye, Sally-O,' for the last time, to wave as the train took her forever away.

Sally saw me coming. 'Michael! Michael!' She broke away from her parents and ran to me. Her mother shouted after her. Sally did not stop, only called over her shoulder that we were going for a coffee. Defiantly, she took my hand. We hurried down the platform. 'Oh, Michael, Oh thank God you've come! They were waiting for me last night. They'd rung up and found that we'd left at the beginning of the party. Mother was *furious.* Dad too. I was so sad, Michael, leaving you like that, disappointing you. And then that horrid row on top of it all . . . Oh, but let's forget them. You've come. Oh, thank you, *thank* you, Michael darling . . . darling!'

We sat down at a small round table in the dreary station buffet, ordered coffee. Sally was on the edge of tears. 'I cried all night long, Michael darling. Darling, you shouldn't have *listened* to me. You should have just taken me. You should have *taken* me.'

The breath left me. Would I ever learn about love? ever understand? ever? I had urged and implored Sally to let me take her, and she had lain with locked ankles. I had given in to her tears, given up, lain at her side, only to have her ask me to lie on her again. Then she had opened her legs wide, had lifted her knees, all as she had earlier refused to do. And now she was saying that I should have entered her, should have broken my promise and her maidenhead. I could have taken her! The thought swelled in me. I could have entered her, *should* have entered her, she now said. How close I had come to love, how close, and I had not known. It was all so sad. Sally went on, 'I wanted you, Michael. I wanted you *terribly.* You *knew* that, whatever I may have said. I want you *now,* here . . .'

'Here and now?' I looked around at the sober crowd, sipping coffee or tea, munching biscuits and buns, chatting. 'What would the neighbours say?'

Sally took me seriously. 'I wouldn't care *what* they'd say. I wouldn't care what *anyone* said.' Sally was her old bold self. 'If only we were staying one more day, Michael, one more *night* . . . Nobody'd stop me, *nothing.* You could do what you want, what *I* want, just as much. Oh, but what can we do now?'

'We can elope.'

'Elope?'

'Yes.' I leaned across the table. 'We can go to my place, strip, lie down: I on you, and you'll open you legs wide as you did last night and I'll enter you, as I didn't do, as I *should* have done.'

'Oh, don't say such things, Michael.'

'You said you wanted it.'

'*Because* I want it, don't say it. It's too late, Michael, too late. How could we elope now?'

I pointed. 'We could go through that door, turn left. Within half an hour or so we could be naked and making fierce, gentle love.'

'My parents . . .'

'They are to the right.'

She seemed seriously to consider the possibility, but then shook her head. 'I can't go with you, Michael. I want to go with you, but I *can't.*' She was near to tears again.

'No, Sally. You can't. I realize that.'

'But I want to. I *want* to.'

'I realize that too. And I'm grateful for it. Don't be sad, Sally-O. It's not too late for you. I was too *early* for you last night. That was the trouble. But later, somewhere in the Cape of Good Hope, someone is waiting for you: that husband you're keeping yourself for.'

'I'm not. That was really my mother speaking.'

'I know, Sally. Don't cry now. You gave me so much, Sally-O, so much. All that you *could* give. I'll never forget that gift of your nakedness, your wide legs at the end.'

I gave her my handkerchief. She wiped her eyes, blew her nose, then looked at me, saying gently, 'Someone is waiting for you too, Michael. Once I'm gone you'll soon find a nice girl.'

'Not *too* nice, I hope.'

'Now that it's too late, *I* don't want to be nice. I never did. Oh, Michael, I'd like to have been that first girl in your life, and you the first man in mine.'

I lifted her hand from the table, unfolded the clenched fist, kissed her open palm. 'You *were* the first girl, Sally-O; the first girl I've ever lain naked upon. No other girl can ever be that.'

Sally bit her bottom lip, looked down.

Then I *saw* her . . . as for the first time, for I was for the first time without want of her of any kind. No longer a white perfection I craved, she was just a girl. But all there was in the world at that moment was just a girl, the whole wide world was just a girl, just *this* girl. My eyes filled with tears. 'Sally-O' I whispered.

She looked up, stared at me. 'Why are you looking at me like that?' I could not answer, only stare back. Now Sally's eyes brimmed.

We looked at one another, just looked . . . for a long long while, it seemed, until Sally suddenly showed alarm, looked away, looked around the room, looked at her watch.

'Yes, Sally-O, it's time to go.'

We went out of the door, turned to the right, walked up the long platform without a word. I held her hand lightly, wondering what had happened in that moment of looking; what had come upon us, brought us for a moment together, nearer even than her nakedness had done.

As we approached Sally's parents, her mother called, 'Sally! for God's sake! Come *on!* At *once!*'

Sally stiffened, stopped, spun about. Turning her back on her mother, she put her arms about my neck, pressed herself to me, kissed me. As she drew away, I could see over her shoulder, her solemn father; her mother, furious, and fearful, surely, that her daughter was no longer *intacto,* a virgin saved for proper sacrifice in South Africa.

'Sally! Come! For Christ's sake! The train's going.'

Tears ran down Sally's cheeks. 'Goodbye, Michael . . .'

'Goodbye, Sally-O.'

'Sally!' screamed her mother. Sally turned and went to her mother, was caught by the arm and bundled into the train. Her father went after them, slammed the door behind him. I stood still, hoping that Sally might reach out an arm and wave. She did not.

The train pulled out of the station, disappeared, leaving only two rails that reached into the distance. They looked as though they would meet somewhere, somewhen, but I had learned at school about parallel lines. Sally had gone, and for ever. And love had not, after all, come.

I walked home some part of the way through the park where Sally and I had often walked in the days when there was hope, even certainty of the coming of love. I was already well acquainted with the ambiguity of God. Since God was love, as was said, I should not be surprised that love should prove bewildering. For Sally's sake I had stayed from Sally, only to be told by her that I should not have done so. Trying to do the 'right' thing, I had done wrongly. Sally herself had said that I should not have listened to her. I should have just taken her, just *taken* her, she had said. If I had behaved 'badly,' we would both have been the better for it.

Perhaps. Perhaps not. With love one never knew; one could never know for sure. Could I even say that love had *not* come? unless I meant only that I had not entered Sally. What was it that *had* come at that small round table in the crowded buffet when I was suddenly without any want of Sally, without any hope of love's coming; when we were both for a moment without pretence; without impatient longing; when we had simply looked, simply *seen* one another? What had then come? Were we truly naked then for the first and only time? Had Sally then truly opened herself to me? And had I entered her then in some strange yet certain way, so that for a moment we were one and whole, in love?

I could no longer regret Sally's going; it was the way of life to love and leave; to let go. But I wished that Sally was with me at that moment, if only to be able to tell her that love *had* come after all, for a little time out of time at a small table in a station buffet. Love had come for a moment, and we should be forever glad for that, forever grateful.

I walked in the park again, walked by my wild lone with the winter sun on my face . . . beyond gladness, beyond sadness, simply thankful for the sun as for the winter and

bare trees, for the bare facts, the way things were, and so for the way things had happened between Sally and me, and had not happened. Yes, even for the way of their ending . . . that death . . . this resurrection . . . the bare trees . . . this winter sun . . .

But oh, it had *seemed* to end so unhappily — beyond all believing — so that I could only smile at its seeming . . . And let real tears run down — O Sally, Sally, Sally-*Oh!*

9 BEATRICE

Long, long she suffered his gaze and then quietly withdrew her eyes from him . . . Her eyes had called him and his soul had leaped at her call . . . a new wild life was singing in his veins. Where was his boyhood now? . . . Or where was he? He was alone. He was unheeded, happy and near to the wild heart of life. He was alone and young and wilful and wildhearted, alone amid a waste of air and brakish waters . . .
James Joyce

'AND YOU, MICHAEL? YOU HAVE A GIRL? HAVE THERE been others? Tell me, if you will, of the women in your young life.' Beatrice Jones smiled from her deckchair in a corner of her garden.

Her son, Peter, had just left to spend the week-end at the home of his latest girl. He had asked me down from London for that week-end, but his girl phoned, and Peter came back into the room trying to hide his excitement. 'I'm awfully sorry, Michael, but . . . her parents have invited me. I said Yes. Do you mind awfully?'

'Of course not, Peter. First things first.' Peter's solemn mask gave way to a broad smile. Then he frowned: 'It's rotten of me, spoiling your week-end. You can stay on, of course.'

'May I? Would your mother mind?'

Peter called to his mother. She came into the room, said that she would be glad to have me stay, though it would be quiet without Peter; she was poor company for a young man.

I felt old in the face of Peter's excitement, and not envious. I said that, after London, I would be glad of quiet.

Peter ran upstairs, came down with a suitcase and was soon away in his red sports car. I followed his mother through the house into the garden where two deck-chairs stood in autumn sun.

I wondered where to start in answer to the question about the women in my life. 'Start at the beginning' said Beatrice Jones. 'Then go on in as much detail as you're willing to do. I love stories. It's been said that God made man because He loves stories.' She sat back, smiled at the sky. 'We have the whole week-end.'

I began at the beginning. I told of my mother, of my early Indian years; of my *ayah.* For no reason, I told of the *sadhu.* Beatrice's eyes widened.

My story continued in an English school; in Ireland then, I told of the gypsy in the dark wood, and of the Priest who was a part of that story. In England again, I told of the naked maid in the attic. I told of Alice.

Beatrice smiled, said quietly, 'Dear, dear Alice . . .'

I went on to tell of other girls whose names I never knew. I told of my feeling that it was only by way of knowing a woman, by way of the coming of love, that I could come to live. Only then could I truly *begin.* I smiled, lifted a finger, proclaimed: 'If you can dare the dark wood of a woman, Ah! then,

> *Yours is the Earth and everything that's in it*
> *And what is more – you'll be a Man, my son!*'[29]

I laughed, but added that behind the comedy of this lay my certainty that without the experience of a woman, I could not be more than half a 'man,' as now.

I went on to tell of Pia Malone. At the end of that chapter of my story, I sat a long while silent.

I took a deep breath and, meaning to continue, turned to Beatrice. She had turned away and was staring into a great rose that hung close by her head. I remained silent. Beatrice sat back in her chair again, looked up at the sky, said, 'Pia has haunted you. She haunts me now. *Having assumed light, he goes again to his place, the Golden Person, the lone bird.*[30]

'What did you say?'

'It's something I once read. Having assumed light, Pia goes again to her place in the world, in the midst of things, a woman truly alone — as the sky, open, unscarred.'

'Pia was hardly alone at Dartington; she was surrounded by others.'

'That's what I said: she was wholly alone, *all one* in the midst of many and of all disturbance. Women in such circumstances are so often only lonely; as some men too; as you at school, it seems, and since. But men can more easily dream themselves away, even walk away — as that naked ascetic who also haunts you.'

The *sadhu* stood once again with his back to me; walked upright and away, climbed a hill of air and, being 'clothed with the sky', then disappeared. I gazed at the sky now, empty of all images, of all clouds, clear.

'Perhaps' said Beatrice, 'women need to know what it is to let go, to leave all that they have ever been; be nothing, just *be.* And men perhaps need to know what it is to stay, to find *where they are* what it is they so restlessly seek; to seek nothing, just *be* . . . For women and men, both, the same *being.* 'Or,' she added with a smile, '*Non*-being. Words fail to tell of the way things are; of the way women and men truly *are,* but seldom know it, hardly show it. Words are always either/or; they're partial, never whole. Wholeness makes for silence. It *is* silence.'

'How can one speak of Being *and* Non-Being, together?'

'How else can one speak of them?' Beatrice smiled. 'Remember Alice's ducks? her Paradox? And didn't Pia ask you to draw the spaces between the wood of the chair, all that *wasn't* there? And didn't you find you'd drawn a solid chair at the end? You have also quoted one woman's wish *to see the landscape as it is when I am not there.* See everything, everyone so: as they are when 'I' am not here. So to be as Pia, transparent, and so to have all things show translucently, with the light not only on things, but in them, *as* them.'

Beatrice turned away again, her head was black against the red roses. She reached to the nearest flower, gently drew it to her, buried her nose in it. 'The rose understands.' She turned back to me. 'But then the rose doesn't speak of understanding, nor of Being and Non-being. Just as Pia, you said, never spoke of love. The rose reflects the light that it is, scents the air it is; is itself, truly, naturally, carelessly. As Pia, it seems. And we — if we are able to receive — are blessed by this rose, by that woman, by any man who is simply what he is, transparently.'

I sat silent until Beatrice said, 'But I'm interrupting your story, Michael. There's more to it?'

I went on to tell of my attempt to be a saint in the east end of London, of my education there at the hands of the thin girl; of the sudden reappearance of the Priest of my boyhood, and how, in response to the Priest's warning against Soho, I went to Soho. I told of Magda. Beatrice turned and gazed at me all the while I told of Magda. When I went on to tell of Sally, Beatrice leaned back again, crossed her thin arms above her head, smiled.

'O Michael Oh!' she said in echo of me at the end of my long story. 'I don't know whether to laugh or to cry.'

'Laugh!' I said. 'For it's all over and done. The end of Sally was nearly a year ago. It's just a story now. One may weep at the time, but in time one comes to smile at it all, at oneself most of all.'

After a pause: 'Michael, you say that your story is over and done, but it hasn't really ended, has it? You've never known a woman — in the biblical sense.'

'No. But I no longer feel so obsessive about it. Until the glad day or night, I'll walk by my wild lone. What else can I do? Well,' I added, 'there *is* something I can do: I can wave my wild and tattered tail.'

'Yes. God save us all from self-pity. But Michael, if it matters so much for you to enter a woman, and so to enter the world, as you've put it — and I can well understand that — why don't you? Better than I you know that there are plenty of women ready, willing and able — in Soho, for instance.'

'Yes, but somehow I need to know a woman a little in other ways before I can know her as Adam knew Eve, as

Abraham knew Sarah and Sarah laughed, as Shadrach knew Mrs. Shadrach.'

Beatrice smiled, then said 'That's more the need of a woman than of a man. My experience of men suggests that they have no need to know a woman, even a little, in order to take them. They know what they want: a woman. It's enough.'

Her experience of men? I wondered but said nothing.

Beatrice went on, 'I speak of my experience of men. It sounds like another long story, but it's confined, almost, to one man: my late husband.'

I wondered on that 'almost.' I had known Beatrice's husband, Major Jack Jones. Extravert, assertive, hearty, he was his wife's opposite; at his best he was Kipling's 'Man.' I had thought this of him without disparagement. Peter, his son, was of the same kind; now following his father's footsteps into the army. Later, he would do as his father: retire and become a successful stockbroker.

Major Jack Jones had survived two world wars as well as uprisings in outposts of the British Empire only to collapse over the breakfast table suddenly, silently, into a platter of bacon, eggs, sausages, kidneys, potatoes and tomatoes.

It happened a few days before I was to spend the mid-term holiday with Peter. We had great expectations of it, for Peter's parents had promised trips to the sea and to London, crowned by a theatre visit. Hearing of the Major's death, I assumed that the holiday would be cancelled, but Peter's mother said that a promise had been made; it would be kept.

I arrived at the front door with a serious face to find Beatrice Jones smiling, slightly, as always, as always serenely. She was wearing black, but she had often done so in her husband's lifetime and, as often before, she wore a flower. A rosebud now glowed against the black.

'Your mother is taking the death of your father well' I said to Peter.

'Is she? Do you think so?' Peter had collapsed at the

news of his father's death but, being his father's son, he soon rallied and acted like a 'Man.' 'My mother didn't show anything much, anything different, I mean. She's always been kind of sad-or-whatever-it-is. I've never known her any other way. She's always been a mystery to me, as she was for my father.'

Clearly the loss of her husband had not added to Beatrice's 'sadness-or-whatever', nor lessened her serenity. Throughout the holiday she was regal as always; as always, a little removed. For all her effectiveness and efficiency, she had always seemed in a world apart. She drove Peter and me to the sea at Hastings, took us by train to London, encouraged us in activities of all kinds; but was herself content to sit on the side and, with still dark eyes, to look on.

At that time and since, I wondered what was the reason for her 'sadness-or-whatever', the source of her calm. I watched her as she walked erect about the house, doing all that was needed with an easy grace, without strain or haste. I watched her as she moved about her garden where she seemed most at home in the world, touching and tending the plants there with more than ordinary love for them; in communion with them perhaps as she had never been, perhaps could never be, with other men, other women. She was made sad perhaps (if it was sadness) by her awareness of the way of life, of the 'tears of things,' since all things lovely are for so little a while: the rose in red splendour now would soon fall in pools of blood upon the grass. She had accepted the heartbreak of transient things together with the beauty of them, so that these were one in her mind, and all beauty was therefore heartbreaking; loss was the nature of loveliness, death the essential shadow of life. Perhaps Beatrice had been made 'sad-or-whatever' by her understanding of this? serene by her acceptance of it? I looked at Beatrice, listened to her and, in this way, tried to account for her: the mystery she was, and of which her son spoke.

I was reminded of Pia. But there was a difference: Pia walked lightly, unburdened, free of the past. Beatrice, however bravely, still suffered the past; still had a future. She was calm, controlled; without the comic opera of tragic emotions, but in no way unfeeling. A woman of incomparable courtesy; her voice was low and grave; her words came slow, seemed well-considered before being spoken; seemed to come out of a silence that surrounded her, inhabited her. Her walk, her gestures, seemed born of that silence; hardly disturbed the air about her. All her movements seemed considered, as those of a dancer in a slow ballet — a 'Spanish' dancer, I thought; with her skin a little brown even in winter, and her black hair pulled tightly back from a central parting into a long plait coiled at the back of her head. Sitting, standing, walking, talking, she had the quiet of a Quaker for whom silence is golden as God.

All, as with Pia, *naturally?* Or did something hold Beatrice's tongue, hold her body?

The morning passed with my stories and the long silences between. At the end, Beatrice suggested lunch. I followed her to pick a salad. In the kitchen, Beatrice added bread, cheese, a bottle of wine. I mentioned that Alice's salads sometimes included wild sorrel, nasturtium leaves, even nasturtium flowers to be eaten with the rest. Beatrice smiled and sent me in search of sorrel and nasturtiums. I also took some of the honeysuckle that grew about the back door. Beatrice scattered the flowers on top of the green salad. For the first time I heard Beatrice laugh aloud.

It was Beatrice's habit to lie down after lunch; her 'siesta,' she said. She went upstairs. I went back into the garden with the book I had brought from London: St. Augustine's *Confessions*. It had absorbed me in London, but I read it with difficulty in the sun and stillness of the afternoon garden.

Beatrice returned, saw the book in my lap. 'Whatever makes someone like you read St. Augustine?'

'In a small, less extreme way, I recognise aspects of myself, of every man perhaps. And something of my own experience.' Beatrice sat down in the chair beside me. I turned the pages to read aloud short passages I had marked: *'To Carthage I came, where there sang around my ears a cauldron of unholy love . . . where debauchery bubbled around me like a frying pan . . .* Not Carthage, but Soho.' I read on: *'In Carthage I was not yet in love but I loved the idea of love.* That describes me. And then Augustine confesses to *plunging amid those fair forms which Thou has made.* That describes what I've *wanted* to do. But I wonder why God made those forms so fair if they were to be avoided, shunned, struggled with? Augustine's lively body must have wondered too, for didn't he pray: *Give me chastity and continence, but not yet?'* Beatrice smiled. I went on, 'And then there's that statement of his: *Love and do what you will.* How does one come upon love which allows one to do what one will — not merely what one wants? Love seemed so simple a matter once. I didn't know it, but it was just a matter of time, of knowing more, experiencing more. But the more I know, the less I understand. Everyone talks of love so that it seems to mean everything and anything, from the coupling of Alice's ducks to whatever it is that moves Pia who never spoke of love; to that love which *moves the stars and other suns,*[31] to the love which is said to be God. But to say love is everything is to say it is nothing.'

'All talk of love is lack of love.'

'I can see that . . . And *still* ask: What is love?'

'If I knew and could say it, it would only be another idea, like the concept: God is love.'

'But . . .'

'Perhaps you have come nearest, or least far from fact, in saying it is *nothing.* Eckhardt spoke of God as *The Absolute Nothing.* That rings true.' She added, with a smile, 'Relatively speaking.'

'The Absolute Nothing sounds so . . . so absolutely negative.'

'So it is, in a way.' She pointed up. 'The sky, Michael: would you call it negative? Clouds come, positively, as it were. They go, negatively, as it were. The sky doesn't come, doesn't go. It *is*. Or, would you say: it is *not?* Words can't tell. That bird now, appears in the light; now it has disappeared. The light *is*. Is light negative? positive? The space in which we now sit could be called absolutely nothing. If it was something, we couldn't sit in it.'

My chest lifted with the wonder of what I could not understand, and yet . . . and yet . . . The sky was nothing at all and so was clear, and in the clear light of it, all things clearly showed — clouds, trees, roses, grass. And Beatrice clear beside me, saying now, 'Shall we have some tea, Michael?'

I smiled. 'Positively!'

She brought China tea and lemon. I said 'Beatrice . . . you seem to *know* in some way. It's not a matter of words, not only of wide reading. What you say about love, for instance . . . If I can't understand, I can somehow sense it is true. It must be experience that has taught you, yet you say you've had little experience of men.'

'What is it you want to ask, Michael?'

'What past experiences have brought your present understanding?'

'You mean *my* story?'

'Well, yes. I don't mean to pry, but . . . to understand.'

After a moment's silence, Beatrice said 'I don't mind telling you, Michael: though I'm surprised to be saying that for I've never told anyone, have never wished to do so, never thought to do so. But, as you have said, it's all past, over and done, and is just a story now. In the living there's no telling. No longer alive, the facts of the moment become memories, fictions, stories that can be told. You've shared your story with me. I can't offer much in exchange, but if you want to hear it, I find myself willing to tell it.'

Out of a long silence, Beatrice began as though recalling an old dream: 'I loved a man once, but . . . And before him, another man — or the myth of one. Girls at school talked of boy-friends and of marrying. I wanted to be a Bride of Christ, a nun. A saint saved me from it.'

'A saint saved you from becoming a nun?'

'St. Teresa instructed her novices: *I do not require of you to form great and curious considerations in your understanding: I require of you only to look.* I looked. I looked at everything — dew on the grass, snails, frogs, cabbages, roses, clouds, the sky at night. I looked, just *looked.* Without thought, I considered the lillies. A priest told me that I had misunderstood, that I was not to consider the lilies *as* lilies, but as moral lessons, a means to a higher end: my Immortal Soul. I considered my Soul. Beside the simple mortal lily it seemed a ridiculous conceit. I went on looking at things, at people, myself among them, at nuns and priests and saints, at the Church itself. As simply as I looked, all simply fell away. Without any decision or rejection, the need to be a nun left me. And much else. In time I ceased to be a Christian. Or anything else. It's said that seeing is believing. Seeing is the *end* of believing.' Beatrice turned her head to the flowers beside her. 'One does not believe in roses.'

I had seldom heard Beatrice speak at such length; never of herself as now. Was this the reason for her sadness-or-whatever? Had she by fearless seeing lost all her old supports: her belief? her Church? even her God? Was this the reason for her serenity? That having surrendered all that was false, she now walked alone, stood alone, without need of support?

And was this where my own wild lone was leading? away from all that was assured and assuring, in the end to walk alone amid *a waste of wild air and brackish waters . . .*?[32] I stared at the empty sky.

Beatrice went on, 'I could no longer be a nun. I now wanted to be a philosopher.' She smiled. 'For my father, it was as though I'd said I wanted to be a lunatic, even a leper. I didn't go to a University — thanks to my father. I mean my thanks. Encouraged by my mother, I read in the secrecy of my room and then, for an increasing part of the year, in my mother's cottage in the Lake District.

But philosophers for the most part seemed content to think; at best to think *about* things. I wanted *things.* And the Indian scriptures to which I next turned for their concern with Being tended to deny the being of things — the lily *as* lily, a snail-in-itself, a dry leaf . . . what Eckhardt called the *isness* of things.

I had not at that time come upon Laotzu, Changtzu and their calm, smiling kind. So I turned from philosophy and the scriptures to poetry, not only for the joy it had always given, but now more as a way of seeing *The life of common things . . . I felt the sentiment of Being spread / O'er all that moves and all that seemeth still . . .* I saw *the parts / As parts but with a feeling of the whole . . .* I read the early Wordsworth, walked long and alone beside the still waters of the lakes, on the heights above them, even wrote some poetry — enough to know that I was no poet. But I could look, could sometimes *see,* and so could be a poet's eyes, as Dorothy for William Wordsworth. As Dorothy Wordsworth I kept a journal, a record of things seen and in all ways sensed. *Things,* Michael. Revelations! See in all simple ordinary things the so-called Christian virtues of poverty, modesty, patience, service, stillness, silence; above all, selflessness — no 'self,' that is, to be 'unselfish.' What is more: things have no sense of being virtuous or Christian, of being anything but themselves, yet in no way apart from the whole. And so are without need of love, of a soul, of God.'

'But women and men can't be *things.'*

'They can be women and men as things are things. Not many women and men walk among us. The Pia's are few.'

'How do I become a man, Beatrice?'

'You can't, any more than '*I*' can become a woman. It's not a matter of becoming, but of seeing ourselves as we are now, and in the seeing, ceasing to be so. See in things another virtue: things do not strive to be other than they

are. Another virtue, unChristian perhaps: They have no wish to continue beyond their time; they have no heaven but here and now, the only heaven. The mortality of things is the miracle of them. Eternity is best suggested by the most fragile, fleeting things — not by any Rock of Ages, but by the little breeze of this moment, by the meanest flower that blows, by smallest children, their laughter, their tears, by birds and birdcalls, the tiny lap, lap of water on the lake shore at night . . . There was aloneness in the lakes, and wonder in the night sky over them.'

'But you left the lakes, and married.'

'Yes, I left the lakes. And yes, I married. I had no wish for marriage, never had. Since I couldn't marry the man I loved, I didn't care what happened in that way. I'd learned to be alone, so that I could be alone even with a husband.'

Beatrice told how her husband, Jack, had been a friend of her father and, like him, a professional soldier. The two discussed wars as though they were chess games. Beatrice was appalled but kept silent. Her father called her a nun sometimes, often a bluestocking, even a philosopher — all terms of contempt. Books — unless military biographies or of history seen as a series of wars — were suspect; books of poetry were perverse. 'Jack was of a similar mind, but he wanted me all the same. I was different from his usual women. A marriage was arranged. I felt neither for it nor against it very much. It seemed to be happening to someone else on whom I looked. Jack took me as one would storm a fortress. No wonder that some women, as Magda, turn to other women for tenderness. I couldn't do that, if only because it never occurred to me that I could.' She smiled. 'I'd read Sappho, but I lived far from Lesbos, in Sevenoaks, Kent. I was brought up to believe that marriage was for life, so that I had only Jack, could have only Jack, however he was. In time I came to accept him and, to my surprise, even to love him as he was: rather brutal in bed, but in other ways a gentleman, kind to his dogs, his son, his wife — in that order. Jack loved to his limits. It's as much as can be asked of anyone. I had to learn, however, to love beyond my limits. Strangely, when I was able to take Jack as he was, I even came to enjoy his embraces, however brutal, even at times obscene. I can't explain that. Why should I? Women in their own way are all as capable as men, able to be nuns sometimes, and sometimes, as your Sally dreamed, to be whores for a night or two or more.'

Beatrice said this. Mrs. Beatrice Jones, mother of my old school friend, wife of Major Jack Jones of Sevenoaks, Kent, once active in affairs of church and town, now a serene stately widow. After the first shock, I began, 'Beatrice . . .'

She turned with bright eyes, put a finger to her lips, then pointed to the old apple tree where a blackbird was singing.

The bird fell silent, flew away.

In the long quiet after, I turned to Beatrice. She was very still. Still listening? To the silence now, as she had listened to the singing?

Beatrice turned and told of an Abbot in a far eastern monastery who came before his assembled monks to preach them a sermon. As he opened his mouth to speak, a bird landed on the window-sill and started to sing. The Abbot shut his mouth. When the bird stopped singing and flew away, the Abbot said, 'The sermon is over.' He left the hall. Beatrice sat back. 'The story is over, Michael.'

'And it doesn't matter now?'

'What matters is what is with us now. And so,' she added with a smile, 'simply by moving from one's fixed position, the world is transformed. So: let's walk in the park.'

We walked in Knole Park under great beeches and oaks into the open. Deer lifted their heads, gazed at the woman, the man, then lowered their heads to the lush grass. Beatrice and I circled Knole House, then settled near a small tree on the high bank surrounding the wall. We lay in warm sunshine without speaking. Outstretched and still, Beatrice seemed to have fallen asleep. I was on the edge of doing so when, with her eyes still closed, Beatrice asked, 'Michael, do you feel you know me a little?'

I answered lazily, 'Know you a little?'

'You said you felt the need to know a woman a little . . .'

Fully awake now, I turned. Her eyes were still closed but a smile hovered about her mouth. I had told her that I needed to know a woman a little before I could know more of her, could lie with her, make love to her. What did Beatrice mean by her question? What *could* she mean?

'Yes, I . . . I've known you for some years now.'

'Could you have any wish to know more of me? *Biblically,* I mean.'

'Biblically?' Still unable to accept my understanding of her words, I looked at Beatrice for help. She gave none. Her eyes were now open, but on the sky.

Smiling at the sky, Beatrice went on: 'As Adam knew Eve, and Abraham knew Sarah and Sarah laughed. As Shadrach knew Mrs. Shadrach and Meshach and Abednego doubtless knew their Mrs. . . .'

I could no longer misunderstand. I lay back on the grass, considered the sky she had spoken to, let her words sink in, rise and swell until the unbelievable wonder of what she had said made me sit up and stare across the park. Beatrice Jones, Peter's distant dignified mother, the Major's stately widow, now offered nearness, *nakedness,* the coming of love at last; my entry into the world, a second birth, a beginning . . .'

'Beatrice . . .'

'Your story, Michael, lacks an ending. You need a woman in order to complete it, round it off. I'm still a woman — somewhat. Whether or not I could be the woman you seek — now that you know me a little — is for you to know, to see.'

'Beatrice . . .'

'No Michael, don't say anything. Don't say anything now or later. The door of my bedroom is not locked at night. Tonight — if you want me — come. If you don't, don't. If you don't come, it will make no difference to our friendship. If you *do* come, it will make a difference for the night, but *only* for the night. I don't want to have an affair with you, Michael, nor with anyone. I'm more than twice your age: two-and-a-half times your age! You seem surprised. I *am* surprised.' She smiled. 'It must be the warmth of the sun, or just the need of your story — it has a beginning and a middle, but it lacks an end.'

Beatrice had not looked at me while she spoke. She had said it all to the sky, slowly, calmly as always; had made no gesture, nor moved in any way. She lay still now as she had done from the start. Her eyes were again closed.

I looked on Beatrice now with different eyes. Her lean body had come alive. She had slipped off her sandals when she lay down; her feet had been bare. Now they were *naked.* So were her ankles and her shins up to the dress that imagination now lifted from her to reveal her thighs, the dark moss where they met, her belly, the slight breasts, the long neck, the austere calm face, the red mouth — its *sensuality!* I realized it now. Had I seen her only one-sidedly? The moon had a dark side. Was the other side of Beatrice's cool calm beauty a *wild* beauty? a barbaric, *bawdy* beauty? a noble savagery now lying still and outstretched in alarming loveliness, as a leopard on a long branch?

I would lie on that body that night as I lay on the earth now. I turned over, said, 'Beatrice!' silently to the grass; without a sound, cried out to the earth under me, 'Beatrice!'

I said nothing aloud. Beatrice said no more. She stretched her arms above her head, swung them forward, sat up, put on her sandals. I stood up, put out a hand to help her up, saying to my great longing to hold her: Not now! Not now! I let go her hand. We walked out of the park with nothing more said, went down a narrow passageway into the town to her home.

We sat again in the garden. 'Your garden is a gladsome thing, God wot!' I said tritely, for want of speaking intimately.

Beatrice said that she would be leaving that garden soon. She was selling the house and moving to the Lake District to live in the small cottage left by her mother.

'The image of a small cottage by a still lake moves me, Beatrice. Such images have always moved me — a Himalayan cave, a hut on a far-away island, on a lonely moor, a bare cell in a monastery; one that requires no religion, no monks even! It doesn't make sense but, together with my wish to enter the world, has been the wish to leave it.'

'How can we leave the world, Michael? We *are* the world. The world is the way we dream it to be. Should we be surprised then at our nightmare world? Can the world ever be different if we stay the same? If we stay asleep? All Brave New Worlds are variations on the old dream. And every wish to leave the world by way of far islands or distant ideals or spiritual ends is the same dreaming. By way of such dreaming we save ourselves from waking.'

'How can I wake, Beatrice? What it the way?'

'There is no way, Michael. All ways are dreams. *Seeing* this is the end of all ways, of all seeking. It is waking from all dreams of leaving the world that one is; waking from the dream of a personal self, or of any divine Self. It is being freed of any greed for gold or for God; being without any wish to become. Not seeking for Truth, but seeing the lie one is and so ceasing to lie, letting go of all that has been accumulated; past pleasure and past pain — all that accumulation *is* one's "self." Free of all attachment, as of all dreams of detachment, one is empty, innocent of all experience, eager, *new* . . .'

She spoke with a passion that made me silent. Then: 'Beatrice, is this what is meant by being in the world but not of it?'

'No longer dreaming, one is no longer of the dream world. One is awake in whatever world one walks in . . . But these are words, Michael, not to be believed or blindly accepted. They are only words unless one wakes and finds them *facts,* not once and forever, but moment by moment. If one is not this moment awake, one is this moment sleeping. One is at most, as the religious and the spiritual, dreaming in symbols, images and words of waking one day, and so not waking *now.* Such dreams of waking keep us asleep . . .

Walk your wild lone, Michael, depending on no one, so that, not needing anyone, you can be *with* anyone, be with all others when they are with you and, when they are not, be without them. And so with all things: hold to nothing and so delight in all things as they delightfully appear. And let delight go if it will. Sorrow in sorrowful things. And let sorrow go as it will. The only hell is holding.' Beatrice paused, then said 'I speak to myself, Michael. You will have your own experiences to prove that experience teaches nothing.'

'Experience teaches nothing!'

'How else could there be continuing wars in ourselves and so in the world? Experience only teaches that experience teaches nothing — until we *see* that experience teaches nothing, and so no longer *seek* experience; simply experience what *is,* whatever is. And walk on.'

As with so much else that Beatrice told, this was beyond my understanding. I said so.

'Don't try to understand, Michael. Let us listen, and let all sounds whether of words or thoughts or thunder or of birdcalls, enter us, if they will, unobstructed by any wish to understand, any will to grasp them. Let all sounds be as seeds that may, or may not, flower one day; may show of their own and in their own way in our daily living. The only understanding is openness.'

After a long silence, I said, 'But surely, Beatrice, *you* are leaving the world in going from here to that far-away cottage in the hills? And for myself, I'm sad that you're going.'

Beatrice smiled, 'If only for your sake then, it seems

time for me to go. More simply: the world I have been or seemed to be, I am no longer. My husband is dead; my son's life and home are now with the army. No reason to stay in this grand house; every reason to go to a small cottage to live simply there and alone. Any wish I might have could only be as yours: to enter more deeply into the real world. As Wordsworth: *to see into the heart of things,* for things, I find, are entrance into that of which Meister Eckhardt spoke in trying to speak of God, and named *The nameless Nothing, the still wilderness;* That, or rather, *This* out of which all things come and abide a while; into which they all go — towards which all that is named Beatrice Jones now goes, as the grey in her hair makes clear.'

Her words were fear in my stomach, a frightening void. Even the calm with which she told of such things, of the approach of death, brought disquiet. I sought safer ground, asking 'Where is your cottage, Beatrice?'

'Near Grasmere, not far from Wordsworth's cottage. The early Wordsworth was, for a while, my second love.'

Who was the first? Who was the man she had once loved? Would I open an old wound to talk of it? I talked only of Wordsworth. Or, rather, in answer to my questions, *she* did, for I had little more than a schoolboy's memory of lines learned under the duress of examinations. She had the poet by heart.

She told of Wordsworth, of the lakes he loved, of Dove Cottage where he lived. I listened as best I could in the light of the fact that I would lie on Beatrice that night; that night would enter her and enter the world by way of her, to wake in the morning (I thought with a smile) a 'Man.' I looked at Beatrice all the while she spoke and stripped her.

With the sun down, it was getting chill. We went indoors, had supper, listened to music after. Beatrice listened. I heard little; desire deafened me. A presence disturbed me, but not with *the joy of elevated thoughts; a sense sublime,* nor any care for *the mind of man.* It was a woman's body I wanted; the body of this woman, near and soon to be nearer; of this widow, sad perhaps with an old and somehow impossible love, but serene always, graciously presiding over dinner parties for her husband's friends, at tea parties for the ladies of Sevenoaks, Kent, for the local vicar and his wife, showing kindness always to her son's friend, always in all ways calm, collected, impeccably dressed . . . soon to be undressed. I tried to imagine passion in her. I failed.

Beatrice said nothing, did nothing to feed or fire my imagination, or even to allow me to believe that what I had heard her say that afternoon had been said. I had asked for Delius's *Walk to the Paradise Gardens.* It came to an end. After a while of silence, Beatrice said that she was going to bed. She said it simply, matter-of-factually, so that I could not find in her words any of the suggestion I sought.

I went upstairs after her. At the door of her room, Beatrice turned, said 'Goodnight, Michael.' No more. She went into her room, closed the door. I stared at it a while, then went down the corridor to my own room. I undressed as in a dream, slowly. Had I dreamed it all? Could I have misunderstood what she had said in the park? No. She *had* said it. But had she said it only out of the warmth of the sun, as she had suggested? The sun was no longer; was she no longer willing to have me? Or had she changed her mind, and by her calm and indifference all evening had tried to tell me that it was a moment's madness, occasioned by the sun and so no longer true? But then she had herself said that we should speak no more of it. She had said that I should *act* if I wanted her. God! how I wanted her.

I opened the door of my room, went to hers. I stood still before it. Then I took a deep breath, turned the handle.

Beatrice was on the far side of the room, in bed. She was reading. The lamp on the table at her side shed a glow over the book, the bed, but left her face in shadow. I went to her. Her hair, no longer neatly pinned at the back of her head lay as Medusa's on the white pillow, black as a nest of serpents.

Beatrice put down her book, looked steadily at me without any expression on her face; without apparent recognition of me. I trembled. Did I trespass? But her nightdress lay at the foot of the bed and her shoulders were bare, as her whole body surely under the sheet? I stood still, uncertain, dumb.

Beatrice slowly placed a marker in her book, slowly closed it, slowly put it on the bedside table, smiled. 'So, Michael, you have come.'

'Yes.' I did not move.

'You'll not come to love in a dressing gown.'

I undid the gown, let it fall.

'Nor in pyjamas.'

I took off the jacket; then the trousers.

Beatrice gazed at me up and down. 'A young man in the pride of life.' Her dark eyes filled. Was it sadness? But she was also smiling, however slightly. She said only, 'I can't offer you a young woman's body, Michael; not a young woman in the pride of life.' She threw back the bed covers.

She was naked.

In some ways it *was* a young woman's body — lean, spare, with slightest breasts, virginal; almost the body of a boy, with hips nearly as narrow; the bones rising high on either side of the flat belly that was marked, as no boy's, with blue veins and a scar running straight as an arrow shaft with its point buried in the black triangle below. Pale brown upon the white sheet, she was not that mahogany girl on a yellow beach I had dreamed of: mango-breasted, bamboo-waisted, melon-hipped. Beatrice showed none of Magda's amplitude, nothing of Sally's promise. A lean widow in an overwide bed, she offered all she had, all she was.

'Beatrice!' I knelt on the bed beside her. She smiled, reached up, pulled me down upon her. 'Beatrice!' I called as I fell between her thighs. After a moment's hesitation, I dared to enter her, heard her cry out, but moved quickly to some oblivion that made me heedless even of the woman I

had so long longed for. Beatrice encouraged me in this: 'Come, Michael, come. Come!' Some great wave of some great sea took hold of me, lifted me up, hurled me down. In some essential way I died. Dear God, I *died*.

I lay deathly still. Then slowly, slowly returned to life and the realization that I had known a woman at last, as Adam knew Eve, as a young Abraham on an old Sarah, as Shadrach, Meschach and Abednego doubtless once, and doubtless more than once, *knew*. I was with these and all other men, a 'Man' at last.

I raised my head, gazed down on Beatrice. She gazed back, smiled. 'So Michael, you have come to love at last? Your story has an ending now?'

'Oh, yes, *yes,* Beatrice, thank you, thank you!' I smiled down on her. But then I saw her eyes, though kindly as always, were no more than that. In books I had read, in films I had seen, the lovers always 'came' together, naturally and inevitably, while lightning flashed over the hill where they tumbled, or fireworks burst over the town where they lay entranced after, equally spent, equally satisfied. It had not happened here. I lifted off her. 'I'm sorry, Beatrice . . .'

'For what, Michael?' She lay still as she had done throughout my onslaught. I saw one of her hands between her thighs.

'You haven't come, Beatrice . . .'

'It doesn't matter.'

'Oh, but it does, it *does.* It matters very much, Beatrice . . . I . . . seem to know so little about love, even less about love-making. Teach me, *please.* Tell me, show what I must do to make you come.'

She smiled, pulled my head down upon her breast. 'Well then, Michael, since you ask, I'll be your teacher — in so far as anyone can teach another such things. I wanted you to come as you did, to end your story. That I didn't come, didn't matter. But as part of the teaching, you should know that it can be bewildering for a woman to be lifted up and left in the air. You stirred me a little and . . .'

'How do I stir you a *lot?*'

She smiled. 'If only for the women who will be in your life, I'll show you. But first lie still, lie down, rest, recover. There's no hurry' she said, putting her hand between my thighs, taking hold of me. 'You'll have me again.'

I lay still at her side. I would have her again, but next time she would have me first. Determined upon that, I lay at ease again, glad with the knowledge that I had at long last known a woman, biblically.

How had it been for Beatrice the first time? I remembered things she had said. 'Beatrice . . . you said that you loved a man once, apart from your husband. You said no more. Can you tell of that first love?'

She was silent.

'I'm sorry. I shouldn't have asked that.'

'My dear, why not? You've shared your story with me, and now your body. As I said before, it's just that I've never told anyone, never thought to tell anyone. She paused, then said, 'I've only lain with three men: Mark, Jack, you. Mark and I were too close. Jack, bless him, was someone apart. I was never close to him, though I came closer at the end. Now he's dead. Now, to my surprise, you've come, and with you something of Mark, my first love; to whom I told everything. Perhaps I could only have said what I said in the park because in some way you brought him to heart again. It first dawned on me when you were telling your story in the garden. It's not your looks so much as your youth, your shyness, your brave dreams, your body now; in the pride of life, as his was then. She ran a hand over me. 'Yes, perhaps your body now, most of all.'

I said nothing. I waited at her side until she went on, 'Mark wanted to be a poet. He got that from his mother, a gentle woman who read Wordsworth to him and passed her love onto her son. Mark dreamed to be a poet himself.'

'Why didn't you marry Mark?'

'It wasn't possible.'

Something in her voice prevented me asking why. I asked instead, 'Where is Mark now?'

'Somewhere in a foreign field . . .'

'He died in the war?'

She nodded. 'When the news came, his mother died; though she seemed to live for a few years more. Her hold on life had never been strong. Mark's father was of sterner stuff. His son's death was a terrible blow, but soon he saw it as a hero's death. He took comfort from that, and great pride. But Mark was no hero; had no wish to be. He shunned violence of any kind, and went to war to get away from his father's scorn for him and his pacifism. His father put white feathers into his poetry books, continually taunted him. But perhaps even more than that, Mark went to war also because of *us*. We'd been so close. He loved me as I loved him. But it could never come to anything.'

'Why not.'

'The world says it's . . . not natural. Certainly it's not allowed.'

'It seems the most natural thing: to love someone and so to marry.'

Beatrice said nothing. After a while of waiting, I said 'You didn't marry Mark, but at least you had some knowledge of one another before he died. I mean, you made love — at least that.'

Beatrice looked at me long and seriously before saying 'I thought I'd take it to my grave . . . But yes, we did make love before he went away. He knew he was going to die. He said it. Once he had decided to join up he didn't care what happened to him. He was sensitive, *too* sensitive. He had no real friends, as I hadn't. We had one another and needed no others. At least *I* didn't. But Mark needed, like you, to know love. In much the same way he felt that he could enter the world only by way of woman, but he was even more shy and never had your experiences. His father was too dominant in his life. Mark dreamed of the coming of love, just as you; and it would have come true once he had broken from his father, as he planned to do. But then the war came. There was no time. Only a few days were left before he had to go, and he was going, he knew, for ever. He didn't want to die without ever having known a woman; feeling, like you, that without that knowledge, he hadn't lived at all. But, again like you, he needed first to know a woman a little. And there was no time for that. I was the only woman he knew in any real way. We had always loved one another. Now . . . we made love.'

Beatrice was silent for a long while. I was puzzled by her story but did not want to interrupt the telling, nor was I clear what to ask. Beatrice went on, 'Mark was no Wordsworth, but he might have become a good poet in his own way. I have his poems still; they're impossibly romantic, but full of promise. *And* full of girls he dreamed to know one day. He was no Wordsworth, nor was I Wordsworth's exquisite sister, but that was his dream: to be a Wordsworth in his own way, even to live in a lakeland cottage where I would be his Dorothy until his marriage; perhaps even after, as with Wordsworth.'

'But he loved *you.* And not as a *sister*. I mean, he made love to you.'

'Some say that William and Dorothy were lovers too . . . Don't you understand, Michael? Mark was my *brother.'*

Stunned by what she had said, I lay silent and still. Not knowing what to say, what to do, I said nothing. I switched off the bedside lamp, held her hand, lay in the dark beside her.

In time Beatrice spoke again: 'Mark and I were identical twins. As children we sometimes put on one another's clothes and nobody knew the difference, except Mother somehow, and she'd smile and keep our secret. Mark and I did everything together. We never wanted other children to play with, nor other people's company when we grew up. They seemed outside the magic circle that enclosed us. We shared our joys, our sorrows, our sicknesses.'

Beatrice paused, then said: 'What is it about twins?

What binds them?' She went on to tell of things she read after Mark's death: how twins throughout the world had been regarded with dread or devotion. In some places, one twin was always put to death — if it was a girl, it was she who had to die — while the other twin was given a piece of wood to represent the dead counterpart. Among other peoples, twins were regarded as incestuously joined in the womb and the link was said to continue after birth, all life long and after death; it was not possible for one to enter heaven without the other. 'Once I seriously wondered if Mark waited on me.' She paused again, continued: 'In Bali, twins were betrothed. I've felt it so. More so after Mark's death, when I also died, and was indifferent to much that happened after. I couldn't have been much of a wife for Jack; at least not till the last years. In Jack's rough earthy embrace I dreamed of being united with Mark in Heaven one day. When I ceased to believe in Heaven, I looked for Mark *within me,* as the other half of myself, as in Plato's myth of the two halves of a Whole that has been severed, and so must seek the other in order to be whole again. In time I came to see that my longing for Mark was symbolic of my wish to be whole, to be *all one,* truly alone. When I understood this I no longer looked back to Mark, and so could at last look to Jack, taking him as he was, just as he was. I was then able to make him happier, I think; I hope. Jack expressed surprise at the change in me. Perhaps he no longer felt he needed to go elsewhere for a whore.' Beatrice laughed, then went on, 'With Jack's death, I returned to chastity and continence. It was not a decision, and in no way difficult. It came naturally. But then you came, and for a moment, Mark came again. But for a moment only. Then it was not Mark; it was *you* in the garden there and, hearing your story, I found myself wanting to be in at the end of your story, even wanting *you.'*

For much of her story, Beatrice's hand had stayed between my thighs; sometimes still, sometimes moving, moving me. I smiled: All essential knowledge should be imparted in this way. Thought should be in touch always. Every judge should have his wife beside him while he judges, and should pass sentence on another with one arm about his wife, a hand on her breast, so that only merciful justice would be done.

My thoughts were interrupted. Beatrice's hand had become more active. She lifted off the bed a little, began to kiss my body, lightly to lip my chest, my belly, and below.

I lay still until I could be still no longer. I lifted her head, turned and pressed her down upon her back. 'It's my turn, Beatrice. You've done enough. Lie back now and only let me know what I must do, and if I do rightly or wrongly.' I caressed and kissed her body, as she had done mine. She began to shift and heave and moan. Then she cried out, 'Come Michael. Come to me. Come . . .'

Her arms and legs were wide. I took my place, played my part. Her head began to swing upon the pillow, side to side. I must wait, I told myself. I thought of unimpassioned things: a calm sea; a midsummer field; that stone crusader seen lying on a cold marble slab in a Somerset village church; that Buddha in the British Museum; that still Chinese sage in a painting there, smiling and at ease on a precipice edge. I thought of the saints: Francis, and Teresa and Augustine, and in my own fashion, I prayed: Make me continent and chaste a *little* longer.

Beatrice was no longer that serene woman I had known. She was animal now; a storm now, a wild sea, a mad woman crying out in the night out of the dark of herself. Then she shuddered, whimpered, sighed, was silent, was still as a puppet with its strings cut. I could now come. It was more like *going,* more like dying.

In time, I came to life again. I looked down on Beatrice. Tears leaked from her eyes, spilled onto her cheeks. 'Beatrice . . .?' She turned her head away, cried openly. I held her sobbing body. Would I ever understand the way of a woman, the ways of love? Helplessly, I kissed her cheek. She turned back to me, smiling now, seemingly only glad. I lipped the salty tears from her cheeks, called her name over and over, held her. She closed her eyes, breathed deep and slow, fell asleep.

I lifted carefully off her, lay down at her side. I had done what I could. It was all one could do. I fell asleep.

As ever, I woke early next morning but, as never before, at a woman's side. By early light I could see the grey hairs on Beatrice's head, the lines on her face, on her neck, undisguised; her mouth pale and unpainted. A mortal woman had given me entrance to a mortal world. Grateful, I wanted to tell her so. I called 'Beatrice . . .' but in a whisper that did not wake her. I got out of bed, picked up my clothes, crept out of the room. In my own room again, I dressed, then went downstairs.

If I did not know how to make love, I could at least make breakfast. I could make toast, scramble eggs, make tea, lay the table. One did what one could. I laid the table and got all else in readiness for Beatrice when she came down. It was still early. I took a chair and went into the garden, sat down and looked back in wonder on the night. Love had come at last. It had proved less than the ecstatic experience I had dreamed it would be. Surprisingly, I seemed much the same as ever. But I no longer wanted dreams. I was sad to have failed Beatrice; sad that she had cried at the end, but I was a beginner after all. And she had also smiled, so that she could not have been hurt overmuch.

For myself: I had begun. That mattered. So much had been done that I could never have dreamed as a part of love. *Love and do what you will,* said Saint Augustine. He could hardly have meant: Love and put your head between another's thighs. Love, and take one another this way and that, front and back, above and below, in all ways, as you will. Love and *say* what you will. In the Beginning was the four-lettered Word, and from it has followed all things, all creatures, all women and men since. Everything was true and in place when true to its time and place. That Word had its time and place: it was a dark word, not to be casually said. It was not an oath, not apart from tenderness as darkness was not apart from light. It was part of love, but of the dark side of love; a dark word, not to be dragged into the light of the mind, even as the roots of Beatrice's roses were not to be lifted into light, into the day. It was an animal cry to be uttered when women and men were happily animal, 'in the manner of beasts.' And only then.

Beatrice came down, dressed with her usual care, her hair plaited and tightly coiled, her eyes darkly outlined, her mouth painted. She was herself again, someone known; no one I had encountered in the night. She said 'Good morning, Michael,' and it was impossible to imagine that any words other than civil ones and gentle sounds could come from her. She gave no sign, said nothing that allowed me to be more than the young friend of her young son again.

I wanted to tell her how grateful I was, how glad, how much the gift of her body and being had meant to me. And how sorry I was to have failed her, to have caused her tears, her sobbing. With a sense of trespass, of not abiding by agreed rules, I began, 'Beatrice . . . I shouldn't say anything but . . .'

She looked steadily at me. I hesitated, but went on, 'Before I say no more, let me say thank you, Beatrice. And say: I'm sorry to have failed you in any way.'

Beatrice sipped her tea, said 'Success and failure are men's words, not part of a woman's thinking. I held you when you "failed." I held you when you "succeeded." What mattered was that I held you, that you were with me a while. That's all that mattered. It doesn't matter now.'

'What matters now?'

'What is before us now: sitting here: sunlight on the table; toast, butter, marmalade, tea.' She raised her cup, drank.

Her calm, her indifference to the enormity of the night's experience, bewildered me, even hurt a little. I saw the hurt, smiled. It did not matter now. Out of the window was a sunlit garden; here was a sunlit table. I took up the toast, spread butter on it, then marmalade, raised my teacup, drank. It was all that mattered now.

At the end of the meal, Beatrice asked 'What would you like to do? It's to be another Indian-summer day.'

'See Shoreham — Samuel Palmer country.'

Beatrice said that she loved that countryside, walked there often.

Shoreham's rounded hills and trees were surely much as Palmer had found them. Beatrice quoted from one of the artist's letters: *Universal nature was a lovely gentleness of mild attraction.*

But I was no longer in a mood to agree. Walking at her side in Shoreham village, in the surrounding country and on the hills, I had come to feel no mild attraction. Universal nature in autumn splendour, fatness and excess, the green and swollen hills and calling birds did not make for mildness in me. I wanted Beatrice again; not her gentleness only but as well her wantonness, her nakedness, her hills and valleys and apples, all the excess of her I had known in the night. The realization that I had known her, as Adam knew Eve, for the last time, weighed heavily.

I was silent as we drove from Shoreham by a roundabout way to Ide Hill. We sat in the pub there, ate bread and cheese, drank wine.

I could say nothing of what was in me to say. I sought the calm of wondering: 'Beatrice, you have no philosophy, it seems, no religion, nothing . . . and seem to need nothing, not even love.'

'Love is not a need.'

Love was not a need! How could she say that to me, *burning* at her side? What was the point of love if it was not a need? What was love for? What *was* love? I seemed no nearer in my understanding. Worse: I sensed that I could be no nearer, *ever.* At long last I had known a woman's body, the actual wonder of what had been only imagined. But, in holding Beatrice, had something slipped away? Love had shown itself over the years in so many guises: it could be anything, it seemed, and everything. But was not that to say that it was nothing? nothing in particular? nothing that mattered and for which, I now learned, there was no need? By way of what had happened in the night I should have come to some end, and so to a beginning. But there was no end to love, it seemed, no end to which I could point. And so no point to love? nothing that could be called love . . . nothing.

The endlessness of love! all without end, unknowable and dark as that sky into which Pascal stared, saying: *The silence of infinite space terrifies me.* Fearful of the silence of love, of the space of love, I turned to say something of all this to Beatrice. With tears in my eyes, I could say only, 'I love you, Beatrice.'

She smiled: 'That's one way of saying it. Another way might be: I love you, Michael. Both are ways of saying what can't be said, of saying there is no need of love. Love *is.*'

'I don't understand, Beatrice.'

'Nor do I. It's not for understanding. But it seems that even science now comes upon a seamless world, a Whole without separate parts; with all things so interdependent, so close-knit, that there is no room between for love. What we call love is the attempt to bridge the gap we create between the separate entity we think we are and the entity we imagine is the loved one. The gap doesn't exist, so the bridge does not exist; doesn't need to. Love *is*, simply, and we are in it; one and all, we are *in* love, as in one light.'

We walked out of the pub to stop at a place where we could see far and wide over the the Weald. I stood at Beatrice's side saying quietly, 'Love is. Love *is.*'

Beatrice smiled. 'Yes. But it's a pity to say it; folly to say what love is, even to say *that* it is. All one can truly say is what one can see: the Weald of Kent, Sky. Hill. Trees . . . whatever appears with us here and now. Nothing separate or apart yet each thing uniquely itself, whole and of the Whole: here a man named Michael, a woman named

Beatrice, who have no need to love one another, being here and now with all else at this moment, *in love.*' She laughed: 'A pity to say it.'

I was silent. I looked, just looked. For a while . . . but then memory returned, imagination returned. Imperceptibly, improbably, the spread and autumn splendour of the landscape seemed to concentrate in Beatrice's thin body, while the sky focussed in her clear eyes when she looked at me, was reflected in her serenity, her grace. Beatrice! I looked at the wide world before me, felt pain and apartness from it, longed to be one with all I looked on, with all that Beatrice somehow embodied for me now. But she had said that we would never be together again, never be one in that way again. I breathed in deeply, breathed out slowly to bring calm and acceptance of the fact that she would not lie with me again. It helped, but not enough. Beatrice! Beatrice!

We started back towards Sevenoaks. Some hours remained before the train left for London, so that Beatrice stopped the car beside a wood where we sat without speaking, until a strange call came from the wood. We got out of the car, went in search of the bird. It was not to be seen or heard again. We walked through the wood to find ourselves at the bottom of a rise covered over with bracken. We climbed to the top, sat down. 'It's siesta time' said Beatrice, lying back in the bracken. She closed her eyes.

I sat beside her. The sun, the smell of the earth, a blackbird singing . . . all, all called attention to the woman at my side. I should be content, I told myself, to have taken her at all; more than once to have been granted her body in the night. I should be grateful for that and not greed after more. I *should.* My head assented, but my body burned. I looked down on Beatrice. *Surely* she must share my want. With the sun so warm, the smell of the earth so strong, the afternoon so silent with occasional birdcalls, how could she *not* want? Beatrice had said that we had made love for the last time, but we had been to Shoreham since, had seen the Weald. I had done the right thing once and a woman had accused me of it. Was I again doing the right thing, and this woman at my side regretted it?

Beatrice lay still, her eyes closed. I no longer needed to imagine what lay beneath her dress. 'Beatrice' I whispered, then louder, 'Beatrice! . . .'

She opened her eyes, gazed steadily at me. Then smiled at my solemn face, then laughed, then opened her arms, said 'Yes, Michael. Yes. Yes!'

I let out my breath, smiled, bent over, kissed her lightly, lightly. The urgency had gone. I stood up, stripped. The bracken made a low wall around us and the wood on all sides a higher darker wall, with only the eye of the sun looking on. I peeled the dress from Beatrice, and all else. She lay back naked, smiling. 'What would the neighbours say?' She added, 'I've never lain with a man like this, in the open, on the earth, in sunlight. I have wished it often.' She smiled at my eager body. 'What would St. Augustine say?' She reached her hands up to the sun, said 'One can never know. I thought: one night and no more. I hadn't reckoned with the sun.' She turned to me. 'I've been waiting, wanting you. Didn't you know?' She spread her knees. 'How could you *not* know?'

Gently, without haste, even without great want now, now that we were together; moving now, now being still, we talked of many things; of love, only once when Beatrice asked, 'You had such great expectations of the coming of love, Michael. Has it been a disappointment to you?'

I could not answer. Near and naked to her, I could only tell the truth. It *had* seemed disappointing. It had not shown itself as I had dreamed it would. That was the loss of an ideal dream; no real loss. But Beatrice had been sad after, had even wept, though she had smiled too. I too had felt some inexplicable sadness — was it that sadness said to come to all animals after coition? But why should there *not* be sadness? How could love that included all things not include sadness? Not being sad about being sad made me strangely glad. Love lifted one up, then let one down to earth where one must for the most part sadly-gladly live. With tears in my eyes and smiling, but saying nothing, I kissed Beatrice's mouth.

She saw the tears. 'It *was* a disappointment then? I'm so sorry, my dear. I had so much wanted to bring a happy ending to your story.' Her own eyes filled.

'No, Beatrice, It was not really disappointing, just . . . different.'

'Different? How?'

Again I was at a loss for an answer. I had been able to talk well enough of the coming of love all the while I had only wished it, only dreamed of it, knew nothing of it. But now? How to tell of the reality? I could tell of the facts: of my body on hers, but that was not all of our being together. What was it that had hung about us? hovered over us? I could not say.

Beatrice asked again, '*How* was it different, Michael?'

Suddenly her words reminded me of the Victorian matron who, at a sultry performance of *Anthony and Cleopatra,* had exclaimed: 'How very different from the home life of our own dear Queen.' I told the story.

Beatrice laughed more loudly than I had ever heard her. Her body shook and twisted with laughter, even to the point of dislodging me. Not quite. And lying on her, in her, under her sometimes, in all the many ways she had instructed me, all that happened now happened easily, naturally, inevitably. A time for all things, and we had time enough: to move or to be still, to be serious or to laugh, to utter dark words, do dark deeds, lightly, darkly, with the sense that love brings of being lived by all that has ever been on earth — space and sky and wind and sea and slime and snake and bird and beast and flower and humankind of every kind, and our own beings the most recent, perhaps the least part. Then, after a long time for gentleness, a time to be wild and blind and uttering animal cries, until at last the still seeing angel in us both and over all the afternoon. Then sleep.

I woke after a little while. I lifted off Beatrice. She sat up smiling. With a hand she wiped some of the sweat from her breasts, her belly. Dreaming of the coming of love, I had imagined it all shining and unsullied. Love had come with tenderness and transcendence, *and* with sweat and sticky mess. How else, since love included all? I reached to my trousers for a handkerchief; put it between Beatrice's thighs.

We dressed, walked down the rise hand in hand, into the wood and out to the car. On the way back to Sevenoaks, I asked 'May I visit you in your lakeland cottage, Beatrice?'

'Of course. In the cottage, but not in my bed there.'

She saw my face, put a gentle hand on my arm. 'I have played my part in your story, Michael. You must not look back to me now, nor forward to me. You said you needed to know a woman in order to begin. So: begin now to live out the life that is in you, and the love. There'll be girls, women of your own age whom you will, I hope, make happy as you have made me.'

I could now smile: The 'Eternal Feminine' has led me on to *this* woman. I think to have arrived at last; at last to have come upon love . . . And this woman gives me a push, points away, says Walk on! Walk on! So be it.

Beatrice continued, 'You have, it seems, played some needed part in my story. I had thought that that way of loving was over and done for me. And so it is . . . essentially.'

'Then why did you . . . ?'

'I've no idea, Michael. Perhaps it was only an idea that that way of loving was over and done. There has been no response in me to other men since Jack's death, as there was none during his lifetime; so that it was with some surprise that I found in me a response to your need, to the needs of your story; a wish to be in at the end of your story of the coming of love.' She smiled and went on, 'There's an order of monks in India who have a strict rule of chastity, much as the vows of Christian monks and nuns. But the Indian monk is also instructed that, if in his wanderings he should come upon a lonely woman with a wish for his body, he should enter her house to answer her need, lest he should fall into the sin of self-will, self-centredness, the illusion of a 'self,' however chaste. This must assume that there still lingers in the monk some natural response to her request.'

'And if it does not?'

'If *naturally* there is no response, it is unlikely that she would ask him in the first place. Or, if she did, he would — being whole and still within — say No to her in such a way that she would feel no rejection, would be more than content with his simple standing there before her . . . with his presence. A man's body might come and would surely go, but the *presence* of such a man, bright as it is brief, would be with her always.'

After a while, I wondered: 'Perhaps I shall return to India one day . . .'

Beatrice laughed: 'Michael Adam, shaven-headed, in saffron, barefoot with a begging-bowl, walking his wild lone into lonely widow's beds!'

Home again, Beatrice went to shower and change her clothes. I sat in the garden on a low stone wall that ran two sides of a small round pond with lilies and goldfish.

A door opened. I looked up to see Beatrice come as another woman: her hair lay loose, long and black about her shoulders, almost to her waist. She sat down on the wall at an angle to me, a little way from me. Spreading her fingers she combed and lifted the hair from her head to dry it, then twisted it about to make a loose coil at the back of her head. With her arms crossed and her long hands lying on the dark sleeves of her dress, she sat upright, staring at nothing I could see; a stranger to me, silent, still, *sibylline*.

I would soon be leaving Beatrice, and forever as far as I knew. Before going I needed to ask: 'Beatrice, I told you of that Gauguin print that hung above my bed. It still does and still asks: *Where do we come from? What are we? Where are we going?* Together with the search for love has been my wonder about such questions. What answers would you give?'

Since Beatrice was silent I added, 'I know that all such questions can only be a game but, playing the game, what would you say? What is the meaning of life? what's it all about? Is a simple statement possible?'

'Playing the game, I'd say that the central question, *What are we?* is the only one. All others are answered in that, or rather, in the light of its finding, all questions cease. Answers are the province of philosophy and religion, but see what little difference answers make in the lives of those who believe in them. It is only *without answers,* without any wish for meaning, that one can live that central question: *What am I?* Who am I? Who asks: Who am I? Am 'I' at all? Don't seek answers. *See.* Walk by your wild lone, Michael; live through all loneliness and beyond, so that you may be wholly alone, without dependence on any answer, any belief, on any meaning, on anyone, however wise or enlightened. Live as you will, in the world as you must, but in awareness all the while, awake to what actually *is.* You may find that the central question is answered by the absence of any questioner. Empty of answers, of all meaning, of any imagined self, you can now live freely and to the full the life that here and now appears as Michael Adam — as a drum *drums,* vibrates, sounds, makes music *because it is empty.'*

'But how can one live without meaning, Beatrice? Why live at all then?'

Beatrice pointed: 'That apple-tree, Michael, what does it *mean?'* I gazed at the gnarled ancient tree, bright with red apples. Beatrice went on, 'You are silent. The tree has no meaning? How then does it live? Why does it live at all? The apple tree has no answers; just apples.'

'But man is not a tree. He needs meaning; else why

should he so long and so desperately search for it, as the philosophies and religions of all the ages prove?'

'Could it simply be because he is *not* a man, simply? as a tree is a tree, simply? Unaware of what he is not, and so unaware *that* he is, and in what way, man craves to become Somebody, Something; wants more and more, wants weighty, complex meaning added to the light, simple being given him.'

'But life without meaning seems so . . . so meaningless.'

'It will do so while we seek meaning. We first assume the need of meaning, then say that we *must* seek meaning. Does a snake need feet? Should a worm seek wings? Does this red rose need red paint? Are these without meaning as they *are,* naturally?'

I shook my head.

'Why then does a man need meaning to be a man? Man, as snake and worm and rose in their own ways, may be simply man; with life given, with sight and the possibility of insight, with five and more senses and all other ways of awareness. Without any added meaning, a man may be a man simply, as *a rose is a rose is a rose*[33] . . . Is that the simple statement you asked for? That — if it is not merely a pretty ring of words — is the end of philosophy and religion; the ending, if it is *seen,* of all search for meaning, and so the start of wonder in us, of being awaredly alive, of living simply.'

I looked at the red rose. 'It's so simple for the rose.'

'And so difficult, so impossible for a man while he remains complicated; while he is not a man, simply, *awaredly.* Awareness is what a man simply *is,* as a red rose is red. The wish for meaning is evidence of the only "Original Sin," which is the sense of 'I,' and is the origin of all his misery, and so of the unholy mess he makes of this whole, holy world.'

'Without this sense of "I" . . . Paradise?'

'Without this "I," where is the need of Paradise?'

'You mean: Paradise as a state of being, not a place?'

'Paradise can appear only to those who are, as it were.

paradisical. And if it does appear, it is as grace, nothing gained. If it does not appear, what does it matter? Awareness is of *what is.* It does not ask for what is not.'

I was a long time silent, then said 'Coming back to the original question, What am I? Could it be said that *essentially,* I am the *Awareness* in which Michael Adam lives?'

Beatrice smiled. 'You could say that. Some Hindus would seem to agree with you, saying: *Tat tuam Asi: That art thou.* But is that only another belief? Like God? Or is it your finding? In awareness do you find any *That?* any *Art?* any *Thou?* Anything other than the real appearance of the world and of Michael Adam who, playing a game, can say anything? And why not? As a poet may say things, make things, bright images . . . So long as he doesn't *believe* in, or hold to, anything; above all, does not believe in the image of "himself." Michael Adam can say anything. Awareness does not say.'

'Awareness is all?'

'All is all that is awareness; all that appears in awareness.'

She allowed me no respite, no resting place, no firm ground on which to stand, no final, fundamental identity, no essential *I* at all. I could stop at nothing . . .

Suddenly . . . at nothing, *I* stopped. In the light of nothing, of Nothing; in clear unobstructed light, there ceased to be any 'self' I could think to be. And yet . . . and yet, here and now, in clear sight and brightest light: things, beings, Michael Adam, a pond with golden fish and lilies, an apple tree being alive, *alight!* Without 'me,' all things appeared as they *are:* real appearances.

Awareness was space for all things; a resting place if one wished to rest, a place to dance if one cared to dance. Awareness was for man as sky for gull: empty and nowhere, a space to fly in; as sea for dolphin is nowhere to be apart, everywhere to be in, to swim in.

But the bright brief moment had passed. I was thinking again. 'Beatrice . . . one last question: Is awareness what the

Hindus mean by *That;* what Christians intend by *God?*'

'Awareness does not ask that question. If, unwanted and uninvited, *This* simply comes, one simply takes off one's shoes.'

No meaning! Nothing! *Absolutely Nothing* but things being things, being themselves, just as they are . . . just as they appear to be. Sudden laughter bubbled in my belly, rose into my chest, burst from my mouth, flooded my eyes, shook my whole body and being . . . Appearance is all that is! All possible wonder lay in the awareness that all is appearance, just as it is . . . or seems to be. Because I no longer believed that my grandfather-magician's hat could have contained twelve doves, I could now delight in the dozen that appeared to come out of it. I could allow the terror of my mother being sawn in half, could happily-sadly now be 'Michael Adam' — aware that that was a real appearance now, and that whatever else needed to appear would *really* appear, even as my real death in time, my disappearance.

But that was another day or night. Today, this moment, *now:* Light! Life! abundant with the appearance of living things; among them, Michael Adam. My laughter gave way to smiling, to wonder, to stillness, to silence.

I became aware of Beatrice's steady gaze. I turned to face her. What was in her look now? What did it mean? Anything? Nothing? *Love?* No, not of any kind I could recognize; neither personal nor impersonal; not of this world nor of any other. Not this. Not that. Not love, just . . . *looking.*

For so long, it seemed, in so many ways, in so many women, I had looked for love. Was love just *looking?*

The question, as all others, fell away as I looked back at Beatrice now, looked until my eyes filled with glad unaccountable tears. Her dark eyes were also glad with tears.

I stood up, went slowly to Beatrice, my hands reaching out. She stood up, smiling, looking into my eyes. In the same light of looking, I held her lightly; lightly let her go.

Beatrice smiled. 'You also asked: *Where are we going?* In a simple statement: Michael Adam is going to London, and now it's simply time to go.'

We turned towards the house, walked silently side by side down the garden. As we went by the ancient tree, Beatrice reached out to an overladen branch, plucked a small red apple off it. Without a word, Beatrice offered it to me. Without a word I took it.

Sitting in an empty carriage, I looked back to the hills, to the woods where love had come. I had dreamed that in entering a woman I would enter the world. The dream had come true. The woman had come true, but I had lost something of 'myself' along the way. It had not happened in the way that I had wanted it; not by the way of some impossible beauty, but by way of a lean widow with a scarred belly and small spent breasts, grey in her hair and other-worldliness in her eyes — a woman who had said Yes! to me, as she had said Yes! to her husband's rough obscene ways with her, and so had come upon Light at once transcending and allowing love.

In awareness of that Light, I could no longer exempt myself from the world, could not stand apart from the world to judge it in any way, nor exclude anything, anyone, not even insurance clerks and priests for whom the world was only an unsafe or a wicked place. It was surely these, but not these only — it was all things and all manner of things. And all places were alike in that all places were *here*. One did not enter the world; the world entered in, was *in* one, in so far as one was not of the world, and so was space *for* the world . . . as Pia's chair, made of space, of nothing at all, stood solidly in space. It did not make sense, but one could sit on it.

By way of a woman, I had come to an awareness of the world that I at once was and was not; of how the absence of myself was the presence of all things, of all beings, animal and angel, night and day, hills and valleys, hawks and eels, snakes, apples, gypsies in dark Irish woods and lonely maids in attics and priests in mourning and eccentric celebratory aunts in Somerset, glowing art-mistresses at Dartington, Devon, and whores of Soho, virgins from the Cape of Good Hope and once incestuous women of Sevenoaks, Kent.

Dear Alice, I'm scribbling this in a train from Sevenoaks, Kent where it all came true at last and not all as I'd dreamed – She was not buxom, teak-brown and brazen on a far-away beach, but an older woman, a widow, wholly and only as she was; and the world in consequence now shows as it is, wholly, only so; just as it is. Just as it is, it's wonderful without being any the less awful – it's awe-ful and ordinary, just as it is and doesn't need to be, as it cannot be, any other way, the way I've always wanted it to be. Don't want anything at all at the moment. Understandably! I'm desireless as a tomcat come down off the moonlit roof, empty of all want. Empty! So that, where 'I' was, here and now is only what is here and now – all London now, coming into view . . . Here now comes St. Paul's; comes here where 'I' was. St. Paul's will go and Charing Cross will come and Nelson-on-high and the lowdown black-knickered ladies of Leicester Square and Shakespeare on his monument there and saints everywhere and drunks and tramps, even Michael Adam, young and old, all here and now in awareness as in light as in love.

Don't expect this lofty mood to last. Why should it? And if this peace that passes all my understanding depends upon the end of desire of women in the world, I'm not at all sure that I could want it to last. Paradox! Meaning, I suppose, that I'm not ready or ripe to be in the British Museum, Buddha-wise, still and unwanting, and so must do what I must do for as long as I must do it – until I do differently. But that's an old way of thought . . . The readiness is all, the ripeness, dear Alice, this Light! Alice dear, this love . . .

I took from my pocket the apple Beatrice had taken from that ancient tree in her garden and had given me. *Michael Robartes* (I remembered) *remembers forgotten beauty and, when his arms wrap her round, he presses in his arms the loveliness which has long faded from the world. Not this. Not that at all. I desire to press in my arms the loveliness which has not yet come into the world.*[34]

But not that either. Not that at all. Michael Adam remembers the past loveliness — the grace of the woman given him, and lets it go. And does not look to any future, nor desire any loveliness yet to come into the world.

I looked at the apple; its red skin wrinkled and brown-spotted, blemished. I took a bite. The apple was a little sour; enough to tell of the sweetness of things, as the lack of love told of the fact of love and how, whether we love or not, love *is.* I bit deeper, ate the firm sweet-sour flesh under, chewed the bitter core, the black pips, swallowed all. Had there been a worm in the apple, I would have swallowed that.

He had been told that life was beautiful. No! Life was round.[35] And as the apple, imperfectly round, perfectly imperfect, good for nothing, for Nothing and for no good reason, *Good.*

God does not exist, but sometimes — when the sun rises out of the sea; when the sun sets and starlings sweep over; when the moon swims in an ultramarine sky; in the light of day and dark of night when owls hoot and mice scream; on a high green hill; on a clifftop of soaring gulls, by a sea into which cormorants dive and gannets plunge, out of which a grey seal suddenly lifts and stares and stares; at the birth of a child and at the death of one; in heartsease and heartache, springtime and earthquake — it *seems* as though God exists.

The absence of God makes his presence felt.

There is no God but how much there is to be grateful to Him for. God so loved the world He gave His sun and moon, the drift of stars; gave sky and mud and snails, small wrens, great golden eagles, hushed dark woods lit by fungus and ringing with bluebells, wind, the wild rose, the open moor, mist, heather and gorse, silence.

A Paradise elsewhere and apart is an imagined one. In actual earthly paradise, the lion does not lie down with the lamb. It leaps upon the lamb; lies down with the lioness.

In the absence of an imagined self, in the still of the mind, in space, in the wide of the eyes, in all senses: Eden is here, is everywhere. The invisible Ground of Being is ground to walk on, lie down on, make love on, die on.

From Charing Cross Station, I walked to my solitary room a long way round so that I could walk most of the way on grass, among trees.

Now in St. James's Park, on grass, among gold and russet trees for the moment (and there is only the moment), Michael Adam walks in awareness, free of 'himself' and so free of past and future, of old hurt and happiness, of preachers and teachers, of good and bad, of the old God of Once. In awareness, 'he' is not and so everything *is* here and now, including the one named Michael Adam who walks, sees, smells, tastes, touches, hears, in all ways senses; at times without thought, thinks; walks on, walking by his wild lone in no way lonely, walking free of the world freely in the world.

The world as it is here and now is the way of God here and now. By way of a robin in a willow leaning over the lake, God now leans over still water and sings to the glory of God. By way of a man's eyes now — any man's, any woman's — God gazes in wonder at the world He is. He gazes so and in such wonder wherever and whenever a man or a woman no longer stand in the way; where and when they walk transparently, *see.* Then the world and all the many things of the world appear as they *are,* as the Body of

God. By way of the bodies of such men, such women, God who is Love, loves; may even *make love,* simply, as He now spills over in the song of the robin.

There is no God, says Michael Adam to the wide clear sky. That is one way of saying what cannot be said. Another way, says Michael Adam to the ducks and pelicans on the island in the lake, another way is to say: *Here all is God.* Here is no Creator, no Being apart, just *being* here and now, always in all ways. Saying: Let there be Light! is saying: Let there be Ducks! Let Pelicans be! And Lions somewhere, alone. And Tigers, burning bright, and Whales in the deep and Albatross on high with wide wings over widest seas in widest air, and Sparrows falling without a care in the world and untoiling Lilies with never a spin and Snakes in the Grass and Trees and Apples and Women *Ah!* and Men . . . each by his wild lone and all in one Light, in Love, alive, alive-O!

In due time, let there be Darkness; let there be Death.

At the edge of St. James's Park, a youth holds a girl captive against a tree. The girl leans back, struggles a little, only a little and only to be able to press her loins harder against the youth. His arms about her embrace the tree.

In Green Park now, at the heart of the world, a woman and a man on a shadowed rise in a grove of plane trees tipped with gold, are losing themselves in the Wild Strange Place[36] while God goes down behind the tall buildings to the west. As a little old lady, God now leans on a walking stick, now by way of her dog lifts His leg to a tree. As a young man now in the pride of life, God runs quickly by. A little ahead and much older, God is coughing and clearing His throat. He spits. His spittle lies silver on the charcoal path. Close by is a worm. By way of Michael Adam, God lifts the worm to the safety of a round flowerbed whose centre is a small rosebush and is everywhere, whose circumference is nowhere. Now God ceases to be green as grass, now comes as twilight, grey. With black wings now and a yellow bill, God is singing in the high tree of Himself.

In Hyde Park now, a tramp, bent and long-bearded as Methuselah, as the Ancient of Days, with bottle-necks sticking out of both pockets of the ragged coat held about him with string and his toes sticking out of his boots, searches around a bench for cigarette ends, shifts through the rubbish of a litter bin.

As Michael Adam comes near, the tramp lifts a wild alarmed head, stares at Michael Adam . . . smiles to see that Michael Adam is no one, nobody at all and so to be seen as another Fool, as himself; as another of the guises of God, even as himself, as the sparrow at his feet as breadcrumbs and rubbish as cigarette ends as the sun disappearing now as night now appearing.

The tramp stands upright. Michael Adam stands still. The tramp shuffles close. With inflamed eyes, the tramp gazes long and seriously at Michael Adam. His breath is sour, cidery, foul. Michael Adam smiles. The tramp puts out a grimy hand. Michael Adam grips it. The tramp grins. Now with one bloodshot bleary eye looking gently on Michael Adam, the tramp with the other eye slowly winks.

REFERENCES

1. Theodore Rosak : *Unfinished Animal*
2. Rudyard Kipling : 'The Cat that Walked by Himself' from *Just So Stories*
3. Walter James Turner : from 'Romance'

   When I was but thirteen or so
   I went into a golden land
   Chimborazo, Cotopaxi
   Took me by the hand. My father died, my brother too
   They passed like fleeting dreams,
   I stood where Popocatapetl
   In the sunlight gleams.
4. Rudyard Kipling : 'The Cat that Walked by Himself' from *Just So Stories*
5. Dylan Thomas : 'Fern Hill'
6. William Blake : *The Marriage of Heaven and Hell*
7. Dante Alighieri : *Divine Comedy*

9. W. H. Auden : 'The Sea and the Mirror'
10. Walt Whitman
11. Arthur Rimbaud : *A Season in Hell*
12. D. H. Lawrence : 'New Heaven and Earth'
13. H. D. Thoreau
14. W. B. Yeats : 'Byzantium'
15. James Elroy Flecker
16. *The Song of Songs*
17. William Chaucer : 'The Miller's Tale'
18. W. H. Hudson : *Far Away and Long Ago*
19. Paul Elouard

20. Prospectus, Foxhole School, Dartington Hall
21. Wolfgang Goethe : *Faust*
22. The meeting was held at Dartington, 1 March 1936
23. W. B. Curry : *Education for Sanity*
24. Simone Weil : *Gravity and Grace*
25. Oscar Wilde : *The Portrait of Dorian Gray*
26. Julian of Norwich : *Revelations of Divine Love*
27. Source unknown
28. W. H. Auden : 'Song'
29. Rudyard Kipling : 'If'
30. *Brihadaranyaka Upanishad*
31. Dante Alighieri : *Divine Comedy*
32. James Joyce : *Portrait of the Artist as a Young Man*
33. Gertrude Stein : *Sacred Emily*
34. James Joyce : *Portrait of the Artist as a Young Man*
35. Joe Bousquet : *Le meneur de lune*
36. Evelyn Underhill : *Practical Mysticism*

It is useless to offer your spirit a garden – even a garden inhabited by saints and angels – and pretend that it has been made free of the universe. You will not have peace until you do away with all the banks and hedges, and exchange the garden for the wilderness that is unwalled; that wild strange place of silence where 'lovers lose themselves.'